SADDER AND WISER

When the door opened, Tiger Lil threw herself at Slocum. Quite literally.

He caught her in those amazing arms and kissed her until she almost wilted.

"Just like in the good old days," she breathed, once she had a chance.

He scooped her up in his arms. "Not quite yet, baby."

But as he began to stride toward the bed—his bed, which she suddenly ached to be in more than anyplace in the world—she said, "Stop, honey."

He did, but he arched a brow.

"You'd best put me down, Slocum," she said reluctantly. "I can't stay. Not now, at any rate."

He eased her onto her feet again, took a step back, and crossed his arms. "Why? You goin' for another buggy ride with David Chandler?"

It was her turn to cross her arms.

"Which scam are you pulling this time, honey?"

He kept smiling that maddening smile. Suddenly, she didn't know whether to make love to him or slap him.

"You rat," she said with a sniff. "You know me too well."

Slocum shook his head theatrically. "Only from sad experience, baby." His hand shot out to cup her shoulder. "Only from sad, sad experience."

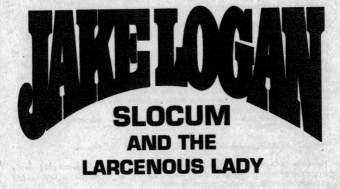

JAKE LOGAN

SLOCUM
AND THE
LARCENOUS LADY

JOVE BOOKS, NEW YORK

THE BERKLEY PUBLISHING GROUP
Published by the Penguin Group
Penguin Group (USA) Inc.
375 Hudson Street, New York, New York 10014, USA
Penguin Group (Canada), 90 Eglinton Avenue East, Suite 700, Toronto, Ontario M4P 2Y3, Canada
(a division of Pearson Penguin Canada Inc.)
Penguin Books Ltd., 80 Strand, London WC2R 0RL, England
Penguin Books Ireland, 25 St. Stephen's Green, Dublin 2, Ireland (a division of Penguin Books Ltd.)
Penguin Group (Australia), 250 Camberwell Road, Camberwell, Victoria 3124, Australia
(a division of Pearson Australia Group Pty. Ltd.)
Penguin Books India Pvt. Ltd., 11 Community Centre, Panchsheel Park, New Delhi—110 017, India
Penguin Group (NZ), Cnr. Airborne and Rosedale Roads, Albany, Auckland 1310, New Zealand
(a division of Pearson New Zealand Ltd.)
Penguin Books (South Africa) (Pty.) Ltd., 24 Sturdee Avenue, Rosebank, Johannesburg 2196,
South Africa

Penguin Books Ltd., Registered Offices: 80 Strand, London WC2R 0RL, England

This is a work of fiction. Names, characters, places, and incidents either are the product of the author's imagination or are used fictitiously, and any resemblance to actual persons, living or dead, business establishments, events, or locales is entirely coincidental.

SLOCUM AND THE LARCENOUS LADY

A Jove Book / published by arrangement with the author

PRINTING HISTORY
Jove edition / October 2005

ISBN: 0-515-14009-0

JOVE®
Jove Books are published by The Berkley Publishing Group,
a division of Penguin Group (USA) Inc.,
375 Hudson Street, New York, New York 10014.
JOVE is a registered trademark of Penguin Group (USA) Inc.
The "J" design is a trademark belonging to Penguin Group (USA) Inc.

PRINTED IN THE UNITED STATES OF AMERICA

10 9 8 7 6 5 4 3 2 1

1

It was four fifteen in the morning.

Slocum was the only one in the place who was awake, and he rolled over restlessly on his narrow bunk.

He felt strangely naked without his guns. Right now, they hung on the wall across the jailhouse, dimly picked out by the first, thin, mote-filled rays of creeping light that filtered through the front window and the cracks in the door.

The night deputy slouched back in his chair, snoring softly.

Slocum was on his first night in the Poleaxe City Jail. If you could call Poleaxe a city. If you could call this rattletrap fire hazard a jail.

And why, when he had plenty of other places he'd rather be, was he cooling his heels in this tumbledown excuse for a jail in a tumbledown excuse for a town, charged with, of all things, murder?

A woman, of course.

A woman who had promptly disappeared once he'd been charged.

Of course, nobody thought that was odd in the least. Nobody but Slocum, that was.

He should have known better than to trust Tiger Lil Kirkland. How many times had he told greenhorn kids, "Never buck the tiger, boys. She'll bite you in the ass every time."

Of course, when he'd said that, he was always referring to faro, which was nigh on impossible to win. The odds were always with the house. And just in case it looked like maybe you were going to beat those odds, the dealer usually had a hogleg pointed at you under the table.

But against his own advice, he'd dallied with Tiger Lil Kirkland and played her game. And true to form, she'd bitten him in the backside with every single one of her sharp little fangs.

Dammit.

A few days earlier . . .

He should have known better, he thought as he crossed the street, making a beeline from the livery, where he'd just stabled Panther, to the saloon.

He should have known better, but she was pulling him, just as surely as a calf on the end of a roundup cowpoke's rope. Her big blue eyes stared down at him from the poster outside the Poleaxe Theater and Saloon. Her frothy blue gown exposed a mile of leg and two round hills of bosom that valleyed into a deep, shadowed décolletage.

And that was sure a come-hither smile if he'd ever seen one.

Oh, he knew better than to get mixed up with Tiger

Lil Kirkland again, but hell. He just couldn't help himself.

He pushed his way through the batwing doors into the shadowy cool of the interior and let his eyes adjust to the dimness.

There weren't many men in the place. Just a bored-looking bartender, mindlessly polishing glasses down at the far end of the bar; a couple of cowboys playing poker with an obviously professional gaming man; a lone drinker, nursing a beer at a rear table; and a single, solitary bar girl, who had fallen asleep on the job with her head on the piano keys.

She was snoring softly.

At the rear of the establishment was a red velvet–curtained stage. It wasn't big. Maybe large enough to hold four big men, standing abreast.

Tiger Lil wouldn't need more than that, though. All she'd have to do was stand there and sing to drive the locals peach-orchard crazy.

"What can I get you, mister?" asked the bartender, who had finally noticed him.

"Beer," Slocum said, and wandered over to the bar. When the keep slid him his suds, he added, "The Tiger around?"

The bartender smirked. "Yeah. She's sleepin', probably. What's your business with her, cowboy?"

By his expression, he didn't appear to think that a man as full of road—not to mention scar tissue—as Slocum should have any business with her at all.

Slocum didn't answer. It wasn't the barkeep's

business, anyhow. He simply took a mouthful of his warm beer, then a long, satisfying swallow. It wasn't the best, but he wasn't too picky at the moment.

The bartender simply shrugged off his silence and returned to lackadaisically polishing glasses. "When you're wantin' another," he added without looking up, "just holler."

Slocum grunted. He was looking at the staircase. He wondered if he should just go up, find her room, and let himself in.

No, bad idea.

She'd likely be with some other lucky cowpoke, he told himself and scowled.

Of course, she could be asleep, dreaming up some new plan to abscond with some wealthy rancher's bank account. That's what she'd been doing the last time he'd run into her.

Well, some women, he reckoned, were just plain rotten and avaricious. However, very few of those were, at the same time, as lovely and utterly charming (and conniving) as Lil.

It had saved her bacon every damn time.

Even from him, he thought, and shook his head. He drained his beer and signaled for another, once he got the barkeep's attention.

He waited. What else did he have to do?

The lady in question was, at that moment, languidly stretching her arms in advance of sitting up. She didn't do it quite yet, though. She nestled her hands behind her head, stared up at the ceiling, and sighed.

Life was grand, wasn't it? She'd been in Poleaxe barely a week, and already she'd snagged the best catch in town. Not for marrying, mind you, but for fleecing. She could feel him out there, dancing on the end of her line, eagerly waiting for her to reel him in.

She smiled. David Chandler was charming and handsome and a widower, but most importantly, he was rich, and he was proud: two attributes Lil looked for in a mark. Because he was rich, he had something worth taking. And because he was proud, he'd be too embarrassed to call the law on her.

That he was charming and handsome were simply very nice extras.

Sitting up, she brushed red curls away from her face and glanced at the clock. Still an hour until she had to meet Chandler for their afternoon buggy ride. Plenty of time.

She began to hum an old Irish lullaby as she slowly vacated her mattress and opened her chifforobe. What to wear, what to wear . . .

At last, she settled on a frothy pink frock, suitable for afternoon—at least, if you were a saloon singer. Lil was all too aware that she had something to sell, and her mother had always told her to keep the goods in view, and the best in the front window.

And then she had the strangest feeling, as if someone had walked over her grave. She couldn't quite put her finger on it, but suddenly her arms were covered with gooseflesh and she felt a little faint.

It only lasted half a second, but it was downright strange. She wondered if she might be coming down with the croup or some such.

No, that was stupid, she thought to herself, then right out loud, said, "Don't be a ninny!"

And then she laughed because the sound of her own voice had frightened her.

Shaking her head, she tossed the pink frock to the bed and sat down at her dressing table. She picked up her hairbrush and began working at brushing some semblance of order into those unruly locks of hers.

Miles away at his ranch, David Chandler was just climbing into his buggy. He picked up the reins, calling, "Send Morgan and Curly to check on those new calves, Charlie," to the gaunt man at the head of the rig.

Charlie took a step back to get out of the way and replied, "Yeah. When you comin' back? Not that I want to be nosy or anything, but Cookie's gotta—"

Shaking his head, Chandler chuckled. Any other time, he'd jump down Charlie's throat—foreman or not—for asking him a personal question, no matter how he couched it. But he felt too damned good right now to rebuke anybody.

Tiger Lil was waiting!

"Sometime later in the week, Charlie," he said,

and added, "Don't look at me like that," when Charlie chanced a dubious—and disapproving—expression.

Gathering the lines, Chandler continued, "You know, Charlie, one of these days you're gonna object to the wrong lady, and she's gonna end up being your boss."

Charlie scratched at the back of his head, pushing his hat forward in the process. "Not for very damn long," he grumped. "Ain't never worked for no woman, ain't never gonna."

"Never say never, Charlie," David Chandler said and clucked to the mare, who stepped out at a brisk trot, effectively cutting off any reply Charlie might have made. Charlie didn't know how lucky he was, because sometime this week, Chandler fully intended to ask Miss Lily Kirkland to marry him.

Lily, Lily, Lily, Chandler thought happily as he drove toward town. Was there ever a creature so beautiful, so talented, so bright, so witty, and well, just so downright perfect as his Lil?

David knew that Charlie thought the ranch was going to ruin, and so was the bank and everything else. As if old Charlie could possibly know anything about running a bank!

And hell, Lil had barely been in town a week. Hardly time for the ranch to fall into disgrace.

Well, Charlie always had been a bit of an alarmist.

Let him stew in his own juices. It would do him good.

David Chandler clucked to the horse, pushing it into a faster trot. The mare, Chandler's Ace in the Hole—also known as Acey—was the champion trotter of the county, and he was proud of her. Proud enough that he'd promised Lil a brisk ride behind the horse.

He hoped it would impress her enough to say yes to the question he planned to ask.

He grinned and trotted on.

2

Having downed three beers with no Lil in sight yet, Slocum reluctantly hied himself down the street to the barber shop. He could use a bath, he told himself, and a shave wouldn't hurt, either. So he settled down in the barber's chair first, the baths being in use.

The barber proved chatty. At first, he was a little too talkative for Slocum's taste. But when the subject turned to the one and only Tiger Lil, Slocum started paying attention.

"Been in town not even six days," the barber said as he pulled the hot towel from Slocum's face and went to work with the lather, "and already she's got half the fellers in town—married or not—dancin' to her tune. Hell, most of the other half's fiddling it for her."

"What do you mean?" Slocum asked and was immediately sorry. He spat out lather.

"Wouldn't try talkin' if I was you," said the barber, a balding man with a bright red shirt partially covered by his white apron. "Them suds taste nasty. And what I mean is that she's got 'em all moony-eyed, that's what. Fred Wilkerson's wife tossed him out on the street 'cause he called her 'Lil' during whatya-call, one'a them private moments."

The barber laughed, razor poised. "Would'a liked to seen that, I sure would! That Franny Wilkerson's one formidable female. Then there's Zeke McDowell. Hell, he ain't had a bath in a year and a half, and all of sudden he's in here every other day." He nodded toward the back room. "Jess, down at the livery, said Zeke's own horse don't know him, what with him smellin' like witch hazel and soap all of a sudden."

Slocum kept his mouth shut this time, but he couldn't hold back a snort. It seemed like Lil was having her usual effect on the male population.

He listened to tale after tale of hapless men acting like fools. But then, he was a little apt to act like a lunatic when he was under Tiger Lil's spell, too, wasn't he?

Still, it helped that he wasn't the only one.

And then the barber said, "Course, just betwixt you and me, I figure that David Chandler has the worst case of it. Lil-eye-tus, I calls it. Why, that man's been comin' to town every day this week, and he usually don't come in to see to the bank and such but once a week. Sometimes less."

He ran a damp towel over Slocum's newly shaven face and proceeded to moisten his hands with witch hazel.

But before he could begin slapping Slocum's cheeks with it, Slocum asked, "The bank and such? What else does he see to?"

Cool, good-smelling witch hazel thinly coated Slocum's face, applied by skilled hands. "Oh, just about everything! Didn't you pay no attention to the signs when you rode in? We got Chandler's Mercantile and Dry Goods, Chandler's Tobacconists, Chandler's Gun and Rifle, Chandler's Feed and Grain, the Poleaxe Saloon, of course, and the Poleaxe Hotel. Then there's Chandler's—"

"I get the picture," Slocum interrupted gruffly as the barber turned his chair around to face the mirror.

David Chandler. He sounded like the perfect mark for Lil.

"You want a haircut, too?" the barber asked hopefully.

"No," Slocum replied with a shake of his head. "Just had one last month. Would like a bath, though, if you got a tub free yet."

"Oughta have by now," came the reply as the barber walked toward the rear door and parted the curtain. "Yup," he said, turning back toward Slocum. "They's both empty. Pay first, and when you're finished, you can go on out through the back door. Unless you change your mind about that haircut. Only cost you another quarter."

Slocum stood, then dug into his pocket. "Doubt I'll be doin' that," he said. He handed over money for the shave and the bath, then walked through the curtained doorway.

"Hot water's on the stove," the barber called after him. "Help yourself. And there's hooks on the far wall for your clothes and guns and such."

* * *

David Chandler called for Tiger Lil at just the moment that Slocum was up the street, lowering himself into a tub of hot water.

After straightening his tie for the fourth time, Chandler rapped a pattern on Lil's door, practically giddy with the thought of her, which was totally out of character for the town's leading citizen.

He didn't understand why she had this effect on him, why she made him feel like a kid again. Oh, he understood why he sometimes was embarrassed to stand up in her presence and why just the simple mention of her name had him erect half the time.

But the things he didn't understand, he wasn't going to question. He was just going to enjoy them.

A vision in pink, she opened the door. There was a broad but impish grin on her beautiful face. It never ceased to amaze him that a woman of her beauty had bothered to come to a tiny town like Poleaxe.

True, they had a fine saloon. He ought to know. He owned it. But still—Tiger Lil!

After all, she was one in a million. Her features were beyond compare, her figure the stuff dreams were made of, and her manner . . . what man could ask for anything more?

"Hello, David," she purred. "Right on time, as usual. Aren't you a darling!"

"Miss Lily," he said, bowing slightly to hide his flush. He couldn't have scrubbed the grin off his face with a bristle brush and a bar of lye soap. And he didn't want to.

"Shall we?" she said.

He offered his arm. "We shall, indeed."

Acey was trotting at full speed, the muscles in her dark bay haunches and shoulders were working overtime, and a lather was beginning to build up under her harness. David let out a whoop, and Lil glanced over—without releasing her death grip on the side rail—just long enough to see him in profile. His face was lit up in absolute joy as he wielded the reins and buggy whip.

Boys and their toys, she thought, just as the longest hairs of Acey's tail lashed lightly at her hat. *But this little frolic is going to get us killed!*

David whooped again, and she forced a gay laugh. At least, she hoped it was. And then, over the wind beating at her face, she shouted, "Isn't this long enough, David? The poor horse is . . . perspiring so heavily!"

Immediately, he reined the horse down to a slower trot. "Sorry," he said, still smiling. "I'm awful proud of her."

Lil barely knew a mustang from an English Thoroughbred, but she nodded enthusiastically and said, "Oh my, yes! She's beautiful. And so fast! Why, for a moment there I thought we'd grown wings!"

Apparently David liked this, because he laughed,

then took her gloved hand and kissed it. "How did I get to be so lucky, Lil?"

She knew where this conversation was heading, but she arched a brow coyly, and said, "Lucky?" as if she hadn't the slightest idea what he meant.

He took her hand again. "Lucky that you ever came to Poleaxe, for one thing. Why'd you do it, anyway? It's hardly Denver or San Francisco."

She smiled and squeezed his hand. "It's the oddest thing. You know, usually I don't play these little towns. But when your letter came, asking me if I might pass through for a week or so and honor you by performing for your customers, there was something about it . . ." She shrugged shyly and cast her gaze downward. "I don't know. Perhaps it was fate."

David slowed the horse to a walk. Thank God. Her backside, despite the padded seat, was practically beaten to a pulp, what with their previous speed and the rough roads.

He said, "You and I think alike, Lily darling."

He reined Acey to a standstill, which left them under the shade of a tall cottonwood beside the road. He twisted toward her and lifted her chin.

Here it comes, she thought.

He took her other hand, and folded them both in his. "Lil," he said, "my dearest Lily . . . would you do me the very great honor . . . would you possibly consent . . . I know I must seem like a backwoods yokel to you, but would you consider . . ."

Lil kept smiling sweetly, but she was thinking, *Get on with it, for the love of God!*

Finally, he did.

And she acted startled and a little shocked and flustered, even though she'd been through this more times than she could count, and she turned her head away.

"Oh, David!" she whispered. "This is so sudden! You take my breath away!"

"Please, Lil!" he demanded. No, pleaded. "Will you at least consider it?"

Slowly, she turned to face him again and said, "I shall consider it, dear David. You shall have my answer tomorrow at six in the evening."

Leave them dangling a little while to set the hook deep, that was her motto.

"Darling!" he cried, kissed both her hands, and startled Acey in the process.

Slocum checked into the Poleaxe Hotel, which was connected to the Poleaxe Saloon by a double-decker veranda, and which sat above the Poleaxe Restaurant. He signed in, but the clerk turned the book back around too fast for him to see little more than a flash of Lil's signature.

As the clerk handed him a key and pointed to the stairs, Slocum rubbed at the back of his neck. "Friend of mine's stayin' here, I think. Miss Lily Kirkland. What room's she—"

"'Hold it right there," the clerk said, cutting him off with a wave of his pudgy hands. "Mister, if I gave out her room number to every yahoo who walked in claimin' he was her friend, I'd have . . . Well, I don't know what exactly, but it'd be a big heap of something like what comes out the back end of a horse."

Slocum leaned on the desk toward the clerk, who shrank back just a tad. "Listen," he said quietly, "I *am* a friend of Lil's. If you won't give me her room number, then I suggest you hike up those stairs and tell her I'm here. Got that?"

The clerk whipped out a large white handkerchief and mopped his balding head, which had been dry only moments before.

"I c-c-can't," he finally stuttered. "She's not here."

Slocum cocked a brow. The clerk was fat and short, and Slocum towered over him, even from the opposite side of the polished desk. Slocum leaned harder into the counter, and the clerk took a step back.

"She's out buggy ridin' with Mr. Chandler, sir!" he said, almost shouting.

At least, it was loud enough that an old man, sitting in the lobby reading a newspaper, looked up with some alarm. "Trouble, Walt?" the old man asked.

Slocum ignored him. "Any idea when she'll be back?" he asked the clerk.

"N-no, sir," came the reply, and then the little fat man peered around Slocum long enough to say, "It's all right, Ed."

Without turning, Slocum echoed, "Yeah, Ed. It's all right."

He took a step away from the front desk. In obvious relief, the clerk let out a little whoosh of air through pursed lips, then mopped his brow again.

Slocum snorted under his breath while he bent over and picked up his pack roll, rifle, and saddle-bags, which had been nestled at his feet.

Hefting the saddlebags over his shoulder, he said, "When she comes in, tell her Slocum's here. Room . . ." He consulted the key in his hand. "Room seventeen."

"Yes, sir," the clerk said behind him as he mounted the stairs. "Certainly, sir."

3

Charlie Townsend rode down the fence line, scowling. Damn that Chandler, anyway! Acting the fool over a woman!

Charlie was ostensibly out scouting for breaks in the fence or maybe a yearling or a calf or a damned mule deer caught up in it. It happened sometimes. He'd hated it when they had to fence the place, or at least part of it. Goddamn neighbors!

He would have liked to blame that on David Chandler, too, but that had happened several years back, before Chandler bought the place from Charlie.

Now, there was a cocked-up deal! Chandler had come along out of the blue and offered Charlie time and a half what the old Circle C was worth. And seeing as Charlie, after expenses, pulled barely more than what he paid his hands—and also seeing as how he liked to play cards and was in debt and about to lose the place anyhow—Charlie had said yes.

Practically shouted it, in fact.

And then, after he'd gotten paid—and in turn, paid off his debts—he'd gone soft in the head and gotten into another game again. He'd lost every last blamed cent of that money in one long, twenty-four-hour game of five card stud.

It wasn't right, and it wasn't fair.

But it had happened.

And so Charlie had gone back to the Circle C, tail between his legs. Swallowing his pride, he'd asked for a job. And oddly enough—to Charlie's way of thinking, anyhow—Chandler had not only given him a job but hired him on as foreman.

"Guess nobody knows the place any better than you, Charlie," he'd said and offered Charlie sixty and found per month.

Hell, Charlie had never paid even close to that to his foremen. He supposed that's why they didn't stick around too long, but he gladly accepted Chandler's offer, and that was that.

What made him mad, though, was that Chandler was making a real go of the place. He'd changed a lot of things—mostly against Charlie's advice—and the place was making money hand over fist. As much as any ranch the size of the Circle C could, that was.

"Who does he think he is, anyhow?" he muttered to his horse, Red, as he reined him around a little stand of prickly pear. "Already owns more'n half the town, and now he wants to own that Tiger Lil hussy, to boot!"

Well, Charlie wasn't going to work for any woman, that was for sure. He'd heard stories about her from the boys who'd been to town in the last few days.

"She's the most beauteous thing I ever seen," young Curly had said, his eyes to the heavens and his hat held over his heart. "Ye gods!"

"Sure gotta pair'a titties on her," Gus Crow added, then cupped his hands a good six inches away from his chest.

"Yeah, I'd like to be hangin' on to one'a them with my teeth right this minute!" Tip Thompson had enthusiastically added.

Idiots, the lot of them!

Didn't they knew that women were all just plain trouble, no matter how spangled or pretty a package they came in? Oh, Charlie had wed him a woman, a long time back. Married her right out of the whorehouse, when he was a kid back in Texas.

And what did he get for his trouble? She'd taken off with a drummer first chance she got, and a button salesman to boot!

Well, he'd shown her.

He'd followed that drummer and his Betty Sue, found them humping their brains out in a hotel in a little smidgeon of a Texas town that didn't even have a sheriff, and he'd shot both of them in the head, just like that.

And afterwards, Charlie had just walked down the stairs, as bold as you please. Walked past the startled desk clerk, walked past the tiny crowd that was already gathering on the walk, stepped up on his horse, and jogged out of town.

And nobody followed him. At least nobody that he

was aware of. He just kept on riding and rode himself into New Mexico, then Arizona. He had a little money, but not enough to do much more than get him into a poker game.

So he just rambled around, playing a game whenever one was handy, doing odd jobs during losing streaks and smoking fat cigars after he won.

And then one day, he'd won him a big game, and he was temporarily smart enough to buy a ranch.

Not smart enough to run it decent, but he'd been keeping an eye on how David Chandler did things. He was learning.

But lately, he was learning that David Chandler was a fool. This did more than irritate Charlie. In fact, he was nearly provoked to murder a couple of times, one of which was when Chandler drove off this morning in the buggy behind that fancy trotting horse of his.

Just because he did a better job of running the ranch than Charlie ever had didn't mean he knew his butt from a hole in the ground when it came to women. There, Charlie could teach him a thing or two.

Especially about saloon women.

Because in Charlie's mind, a woman who sang in a bar was the same as a woman who worked on her back in one. And there was no way he was going to let another hussy come ruin his life, no matter what capacity she arrived in!

Charlie whoaed his horse. There, stuck in the fence, was a hapless mule deer doe. It had given up struggling against the wires that tangled its legs and just lay there, panting heavily.

Charlie pulled his rifle, aimed, and fired, then rode on past the now-still corpse.

It felt damn good to kill something.

Damn good.

David and Lily arrived back at the saloon/hotel around suppertime. Lily had been coy all afternoon about the marriage proposal, but being a gentleman, he didn't press her.

She had said tomorrow at six, and tomorrow at six it would be.

If she didn't answer him then, he'd go crazy.

He rounded the buggy, tying Acey at the rail on his way, then helped her down.

"Always so polite, David," she said demurely.

"Always at your service, ma'am," he said, smiling. He gave her a wink and hoped she knew that he really meant that *always* part.

He offered his arm and escorted her into the lobby, where she asked for her key before he had a chance to do it for her. Well, he supposed she was accustomed to being on her own.

That was one reason he loved her: her independence. It was incredibly refreshing after all these wilting wallflowers that seemed to populate the territory.

"Miss Lil, ma'am?" stuttered Walt, the desk clerk, as he handed over her key. Walt was still in awe of her, as he supposed was most of the town.

"Yes, Walter?" she said, smiling.

Which only served to make Walt's discomfort worse. But he managed to blurt, "A man named Slocum says to tell you he's in number seventeen."

Slocum? Who was Slocum?

Lil seemed puzzled, too, much to David's relief. She tipped her head and knitted her brow, and said, "What is this gentleman's name again?"

Walt repeated it, and Lil shook her head. "Doesn't ring any bells." She turned toward David, a smile on her lips. "Things like this happen all the time. I'm sure you understand, darling."

That *darling* almost had David's knees knocking. "Of course I do, Lily. Just a fan, I'm certain. If he gives you any trouble, I can assure you that—"

She laughed, and it was like music. "Dear David, I've dealt with his kind before and never come to any harm. But I shall keep you in mind." She put a hand to the side of his face and added, "My knight in shining armor."

David felt a hot flush creeping up his neck. "I suppose I'd best take my rig to the stable," he said lamely.

"You'll be there for my first show?" she asked, one dainty foot on the first riser of the stairs.

"Certainly!" he said. "And I expect to buy your dinner at the hotel between the first and the second performances."

"As always," she purred.

He doffed his hat. "Until later, my love," he said. And left to take Acey down to Jess's livery stable.

As the owner, David had his own private suite at the hotel, and he wondered, as he handed over the rig to Jess, if perhaps he should invite Lil up for a quiet supper for two this evening.

When she was through working, of course. He had more in mind than food.

But he decided against it.

Lil was a lady, after all. She might not take kindly to any premarital advances he might make. No, he'd best be patient and hold off till the wedding.

He was already convinced that she'd say yes and make him the happiest man in the territory.

Tiger Lil took dainty, ladylike steps until she was out of Walt's earshot, then hurried to her room. It was a corner room and faced both the street and the saloon, and she wanted to make certain that David was indeed on his way to the stable.

When she saw his rig out in front of it, far down the street, she turned on her heel and stormed out and down the hall to number seventeen.

She pounded on the door.

When it opened, she threw herself at Slocum. Quite literally.

He caught her in his amazing arms and kissed her until she almost wilted.

"Just like the good old days," she breathed, once she had a chance.

He scooped her up in his arms. "Not quite yet, baby."

But as he began to stride toward the bed—his bed, which she suddenly ached to be in more than anyplace in the world—she said, "Stop, honey."

He did, but he arched a brow.

"You'd best put me down, Slocum," she said reluctantly. "I can't stay. Not now, at any rate."

He eased her onto her feet again, took a step back, and crossed his arms. "Why? You goin' for another buggy ride with David Chandler?"

It was her turn to cross her arms. "You seem to know a great deal for a man who just rode into town."

He smiled at her. Oh, God, how she wanted to rush back into his embrace, into his bed, to feel his hands, his lips, on her body once more, feel him inside her once again.

It had been far too long.

He said, "Easy enough to find out when the citizens are volunteerin' information so free and easy. You're the talk of the town, Lily."

She shrugged. Maybe tonight, after her second show . . .

"Which scam are you pulling this time, honey?"

Immediately, she stuck her nose in the air. "Why, I'm quite sure I don't know what you're talking about!"

He kept smiling that maddening smile. Suddenly, she didn't know whether to make love to him or slap him.

He said, "You're blushing, Lil."

"You rat," she said with a sniff. "You know me too well."

Slocum shook his head theatrically. "Only from sad experience, baby." His hand shot out to cup her shoulder. "Only from sad, sad, experience."

Again, she felt torn between telling him where to get off and practically raping him. But she had to keep her senses about her. There was too much at stake.

Gently, she swept his hand away and took a step back, separating them even farther.

"Come to my second show tonight, Slocum. After, we can . . . talk."

Slocum nodded.

"But if you see me before, or in anyplace public, I'll scream for help," she said. "Count on it."

"This Chandler must be some kind of mark," Slocum said.

"He is indeed," she said, then slipped out the door.

Once she got back to her room, she had to lean against her closed door just to stay on her feet.

Who would think that a man she hadn't seen for almost two years could shake her so?

But he had, hadn't he?

Even after she'd treated him so shabbily in Sacramento! She'd almost felt bad about it, running out on him, leaving him with her mess to clean up.

But it didn't seem as if he held a grudge. Slocum wouldn't.

If he weren't so itchy-footed, and she weren't so—all right—larcenous, she might have considered marrying him. She knew he could keep her happy in bed like no other man she'd met.

Sighing, she at last moved away from the door and lay down on her bed. The clock hanging on the opposite wall told her she had two hours until the first show. That would have been plenty of time to be with Slocum, even though she doubted they could have held it down to just once or twice.

But she couldn't go to David smelling of Slocum, smelling of lovemaking, and expect that he wouldn't notice. It took a good hour to get her bathwater brought up in this backwater dump.

She sighed again and loosened her bodice. She'd go to Slocum later, once she'd had her usual nap, sung, had dinner with David, sung again, then bade David good night. A chaste good night, she hoped.

She drifted off with a smile on her lips, thinking about the evening to come.

4

Slocum waited until her footsteps faded and he heard the door close behind her, down the hall, and then he nearly put his fist through the wall.

That helped divert his attention from his fading erection, but it did little good for the wall. He shoved the bureau over a few inches to cover the dent he'd made in the cheap wallpaper—and the plaster behind it.

Why did she have this effect on him?

It was like he was loco when he was around her, loco at the mere mention of her name. And now he'd have to wait until probably eleven, maybe midnight, to get her into his bed.

He'd forgotten to ask when her last show was over, dammit.

He ought to leave town now.

He should go straight down to the livery, pack up his horse, and ride as far and as fast as he could until nightfall. He knew this, but he didn't do it.

He couldn't do it.

All he could do was sink down in the room's single chair, hoist his boots up on the bed, and mutter, "Well, shit!"

*   *   *

David Chandler arrived just in time for the first show and settled in at his table, right up next to the stage. He crooked his finger at the bartender, and at just about the time that a mug of beer was deposited in front of him, the curtains opened.

The whole room—which was packed practically to the rafters—exploded in raucous applause and whistles. No catcalls, though, he noted with a brief grin. The boys in town respected his Lil too much.

She was a lady.

He felt a swell of pride as she walked out on the stage and curtsied to the crowd, then held up her hands, calling, "Don't make me sing over you, fellas!"

The crowd immediately quieted, and standing there in her red dress, her plump breasts straining at her low-cut bodice, she clasped her hands before her and sang "Amazing Grace" without benefit of accompaniment.

And she was right on key.

When she finished, the hushed, almost reverent crowd burst into another round of applause and cheers. And why wouldn't they? Her voice was as smooth and sweet as clover honey, and as moving and strong as a wild bull. It was an incredible combination in one little woman.

She held up her hands again, smiling, and once the room quieted again, she nodded to the piano player and laughed into a spirited version of "Three Cheers for Billy," always a crowd pleaser.

She kept on singing—and dancing, sometimes—for a full half hour before she closed the performance with another quiet, religious number—"Ave Maria"—for which she put away her bag of tricks and struts and high kicks and resumed a demure, reverent pose.

The room went wild as she left the stage, only to return three times for extra bows. Men threw flowers and gold pieces at the stage and shouted, "I love you, gal!" but his Lily only smiled.

And then the curtains closed, and the room grudgingly went back to its normal low rumble of conversation. The roulette wheel began to turn and rattle again, card games resumed, and men regained their senses enough to belly up to the bar once more.

David heaved a happy sigh, then pushed back from the table, leaving his beer untouched. He'd forgotten it. He always ordered one with the intention of sipping at it and always completely forgot it was there once Lil came onstage.

She just had that sort of effect on him.

And he liked it. He didn't remember ever having liked anything so much: not cutting that big deal—the mother of all deals!—with Tan Thurber up in Ohio, not holding up the First National Bank of Cincinnati, not even locking Thurber and his ratty gang of thugs in that little backwoods shed of theirs and setting fire to it.

He'd sat outside, listening to the screams. And he'd whistled to their cries of pain and rage and impotence, because the whole hundred thousand and change was nestled safe in the valise strapped to his saddle.

But even that was nothing compared to the absolute thrill of Tiger Lil.

He'd die for her.

He'd kill for her.

Grinning unconsciously, he made his way through the crowd and out the side door, then down the long double porch to the stage entrance. He went inside and took a few steps down the hall toward a fan of light spreading across the floorboards.

He stopped at the door from under which it issued, waited a moment, then smiling, he rapped at her dressing room door.

"Ready, my darling?" he called. "I hope you have a good appetite!"

Slocum had been outside, sitting on the porch, when David Chandler left the hotel for the saloon. He knew it was David Chandler because a neatly dressed man had come up to him and tipped his hat. "Evening, Mr. Chandler," he'd said.

But Slocum knew David Chandler the moment he saw him. Not as David Chandler, though.

About seven years back, when he was up in Nebraska, Slocum had gotten into a poker game that included Red Eye O'Neill, a couple of farmers, the town undertaker, and a gent named Felix Hamilton. Nobody won really big at that game, but Slocum remembered it because of what happened right after.

He remembered Hamilton's head coming up quick when a new man entered the bar. Hamilton knocked over a drink right away to cover it, but Slocum had seen. Hamilton muttered something about ruining his new pants and stood up. Slocum and old Red Eye eyed each other. Red Eye had been paying attention, too.

But before Slocum and Red Eye had more than the chance to stare at each other and figure that trouble was coming, Hamilton drew his sidearm and fired three quick shots into the back of the bar's new patron.

Slocum had tried to draw his gun, but one of the farmers between him and Hamilton panicked and bowled him over. He'd hit his head, hard, on the way down, and the lights went out, as they say.

Red Eye hadn't been so lucky. Slocum was told later that Red Eye had drawn on Hamilton, but Hamilton's gun was already out, and his bloodlust was up. He'd shot Red Eye through the heart before he'd even had a chance to clear leather, then turned to the undertaker.

"There," he'd said. "Two instead of one, maybe three if that tall son of a gun hit his head hard enough. I hope you're grateful I threw you some extra business."

After which, he simply walked out of the saloon, got on his horse, and jogged out of town, pretty as you please.

Which had been enough to get Slocum up out of bed and on Hamilton's trail.

But he'd lost the goddamn horse's turd. It was as if he had just vanished, like an early morning canyon mist.

It had bothered Slocum ever since.

In fact, David Chandler had been luckier than he knew that Slocum hadn't just fired from the shadows and called it even.

But Slocum hadn't.

He sat out on the porch, listening to Lily sing, while he puzzled it over.

What was a gunman like Hamilton—or Chandler—doing in a place like this? Why had he settled down, bought property and plenty of it? Shootists and thieves like Chandler usually had itchy feet, or learned to develop them to stay one step ahead of the law.

Also, they didn't buy things. They stole them.

And more importantly, why was he snooping around Lily?

He already knew why Lil was snooping around Chandler. He also figured she couldn't possibly be aware of just how dangerous he could be.

But now wasn't the time to tell her. Especially now, he thought, when she stopped singing and the final, lingering applause traveled out to him. He knew

Chandler was in the bar, part of the crowd, and he didn't trust the man to have changed his ways.

Once a killer, always a killer.

A little while later, he heard voices on the walk. Lil and Chandler were approaching him, and he pulled his hat down to shade his face from the lamp flickering on its hook.

They walked on past without pausing, although he knew Lil would have known it was him—from his size and build, if nothing else.

Slocum was bigger than most men.

He waited in his chair until they went into the restaurant, and then he stood up, casually stretched his arms, and sauntered on over to the saloon. He owed Chandler for old Red Eye's sake. Red Eye would have wanted it that way.

He did, too.

When David and Lil returned from dinner—over which he had been a perfect gentleman, for which she was grateful—he dropped her at her dressing room door, then bowed.

"I'll be in my usual place," he said, all charm. And all money.

Normally, she liked her men more rugged, Slocum being a prime example. But when a mark had the money, charm, money, looks, money, courtliness, and money—had she mentioned money?—of a David Chandler, there was no question as to which she'd pick.

To swindle, at least.

She'd been to the altar five times in her twenty-six years. She'd been close to it a great many more times than that. And with few exceptions, things had turned out in her favor.

Even on those occasions when they didn't, she always managed to come out smelling like a rose, although it might have been a rose freshly transplanted to another state or territory.

Lucky, she thought as she touched up her hair and makeup. *I'm just plain lucky.*

But when her clock told her it was time for her second (and last) show of the evening, she put down her brush, stood up from the dressing table, eased a red feather boa from the place where it always hung—over her dressing screen—and squared her shoulders. She thrust out her bosom and sucked in her stomach.

"Showtime," she whispered with a smile.

Tomorrow she was going to cook David Chandler's goose, and he wouldn't know that he'd been plucked, stuffed, stuck in the oven, basted, and served up for supper until it was far too late.

She started down the hall toward the stage.

And ran right into none other than Slocum.

Her first instinct was to be angry with him, but her insides were melting like honeycomb suddenly thrust into a fire. She couldn't help it.

He leaned against the wall, lighting a smoke, and

the flame of his lucifer washed up over his face, bright and golden.

He spoke, his tone low and intimate. "Sing 'Lorena' tonight, Lily. For me."

And then he stepped out of her path. She brushed past him without a word, but she knew that the color she felt burning brightly in her cheeks told him everything he wanted to know.

In fact, as she reached the edge of the stage, its curtains still drawn, she heard him chuckle back there in the darkness.

Damn his ornery hide anyway! Why did he have to turn up at this particular moment, when she had the prize catch of all time circling so close to her hook?

And why did he have to have such a mesmerizing effect on her?

She could feel his patient and practiced hands on her bare, pale skin now, even though he was a good fifteen feet behind her.

The curtain opened, revealing the light from the stage lanterns. The cheering began.

She let it go on for a moment while she regained her composure and then stepped out onto the stage. She gave a low curtsy, then waited.

When the crowd quieted at last, she didn't sing the tune that she usually sang every night to open the second show. Instead, she opened her mouth and began to warble, with a slow, silky, sultry tone that was full of heartache and loneliness and longing, "The years creep slowly by, Lorena / The snow is on the grass again . . ."

From the corner of her eye, she saw that Slocum had come out and was standing by the bar. He winked at her, and she immediately turned her attention to David, who sat at her feet, puzzled but rapt.

"The sun's low down the sky, Lorena / The frost gleams where the flowers have been . . ."

An old man began to openly weep as she sang the old Civil War favorite—a favorite of both sides.

Several others bowed their heads, one genuflected, and she saw more than one handkerchief at work in the back of the room. Slocum gave good advice. He knew how she should work a crowd, all right.

She continued singing, hands clasped before her, making the song more plaintive and poignant than she believed she'd ever sung it before.

As is the habit of most ranch hands, whose days start before the sun has risen, Charlie had turned in early.

He lay in his bunk in the little foreman's cottage that David Chandler had built for him. Crazy idea that. Waste of money. He'd never built any such thing when he'd owned the Circle C, although he had to admit he didn't much admire the thought of sharing quarters with men who'd known him as owner before his sudden and humiliating drop in rank.

But he couldn't sleep, although the bed was comfortable. Too soft, he always said—at least to himself—for a working man.

He tossed and turned, and all he could think about was how Chandler was making a fool of himself with that woman. The way Charlie thought of her, it ought to be in capital letters: That Woman.

More like That Damned Woman.

There wasn't a single thing Charlie held in favor of these current goings-on. He didn't like women. Noisy, rattlesome things, the lot of them; always dusting where you wanted to put your elbow or harping at you to wipe your boots or take off your spurs in the house, the best of them. He wouldn't be able to stand a woman on the place—especially her.

She'd either take over the place entirely, or more likely, rob Chandler blind and run off in the night with some drummer.

Chandler was an idiot.

Now, even though David Chandler had been nothing but good to him, Charlie couldn't help but resent it, and not just a little. It fairly oozed from his pores.

Charlie had a checkered past, but he was a proud old rooster. He wasn't about to tolerate some fancy-feathered hen coming in and turning his world upside down, no matter how beautiful or charming or big tittied the boys said she was, no sir.

He'd given serious consideration to just riding out, himself. But that wasn't enough, somehow. It didn't make a whatyacall . . . statement.

He'd also thought of riding straight into town and just shooting That Woman right through her head. It's what he'd done to his own wife, and he'd do it without a second's thought.

He rolled over and tried to get some sleep. Maybe the sixth or seventh time was the charm, he thought with a snort.

There was nothing he could do tonight, anyhow, except stew in his own juices.

5

David walked Lily back to the hotel room and left her at her door. He kissed the palm of her hand before he said good night.

"Until tomorrow," he said before he softly closed the door between them.

Lil plopped down on her mattress and heaved a sigh. Should she? Shouldn't she?

Of course, she shouldn't! She should tell Slocum to meet her next week, next month, whenever her business here was done and tied with a neat ribbon. And she had a good-sized chunk of David Chandler's money.

But although Lily was a woman of great restraint when necessary—and a consummate actress, at least when she was singing, or when she was working a mark—she realized there was one thing—one man—she couldn't resist. And that man saw through her as clearly as if she were made of glass.

Maybe that was the source of her attraction.

Or, she thought with a little shrug, maybe it was just lust, plain and simple.

A shiver of desire passed through her, and she stood on shaking legs. Damn it, anyway! Should or shouldn't? It didn't make any difference.

She went to her bureau and pulled the pins from her hair, brushing it until it hung down over her shoulders and cascaded down her back like soft, red waves. Quickly, she took off her dress, laid it out carefully, and then went to work on her underthings.

When she was finished, she donned a frothy negligee, a soft baby blue one that she knew set off her hair and eyes. And that she'd been saving for her wedding night with David.

Well, he'd just have to take seconds, that was all. In fact, she hadn't given him a thought since she started stripping the pins from her hair.

Her mouth quirked up in a secret smile.

Giving her hair a final brush over her shoulder with her fingers, she opened the door and peered out into the hall.

It was empty, and she smiled.

Softly, she started padding toward Slocum's room.

At his door, she knocked softly.

No answer.

Brow knitted, she gave a harder rap with her knuckles.

Nothing.

Angrily, she tried the latch.

Locked!

Where the hell was he?

Livid, a frustrated Lily stalked back to her room, where numerous pieces of the management's bric-a-brac were about to meet their doom.

*   *   *

Slocum stood in the shadows of an overhang and peered curiously through the bank manager's office window. The object of his attention was David Chandler, who, by the light of a single desk lamp, seemed to be fiddling with an entry ledger.

And by fiddling, Slocum meant just that. Chandler appeared to be changing entries here and there. Even from the outside, with the glass between them, Slocum could hear him whistling softly. And happily, too, it sounded like.

Slocum figured that he knew what Chandler was up to, but why?

Why would a man steal from his own damn bank?

Did he swipe stuff from the shelves of his mercantile, too, and hide them under his coat, away from the manager's eyes? It was a puzzlement, that was for sure.

Slocum had been in his hotel room, waiting for Lil, but when Chandler left her at her door, he walked back the other way, toward the stairs, and Slocum determined to follow him. Lily was going to be madder than a bag full of badgers, but it was for her own good.

Not that she'd be appreciative of it right away. In fact, she'd probably lay into him pretty good.

But then, she was at her best when she was mad, wasn't she?

He smiled, and just then, Chandler blew out the lamp on the desk. Slocum backed farther into the shadows, in case Chandler was suspicious. He'd be able to see outside, now that the light was out.

But he didn't come to the window. Slocum watched, sidling around the building, as Chandler—or rather the hint of a shadow that was him—walked out into the main bank, then back behind the teller's cage. He stopped and seemed to be fumbling for something in his pocket. It turned out to be a lucifer.

Chandler struck it, then leaned toward the wall, which Slocum had just realized wasn't the wall but the face of the safe. By the light of his sulfur tip, Chandler carefully turned the dial this way and that, and then opened the safe door.

It was a big safe, because he walked inside. More like a vault, Slocum thought. And then he thought it was odd that a little town like Poleaxe would have a need for such a thing.

Chandler came out as quickly as he had gone inside. Tucking something into his inside coat pocket, he closed and locked the safe behind him. At least Slocum thought so. Chandler's match had gone out, and everything was shadows again.

So, just what had he taken out of there? Cash? Paper money?

Maybe he was stealing something out of the safe-deposit boxes, if this hick town had such a thing.

Quietly, Slocum backed around the corner of the building when Chandler's shadow approached the front door. Whatever he'd been up to in there, he was finished, because he came out on the walk, then locked the door behind him. As he strode back down toward the hotel, Slocum followed him.

But all Chandler did was go up the stairs and sup-
posedly to his room. At least, he walked down to the
far end of the hall and entered a door there.

"Shit," Slocum whispered. He was annoyed. He'd
hoped that he'd have some excuse to shoot Chandler,
or at least knock him out.

Well, he hadn't really. Not tonight, anyway, and
not in town. Chandler practically owned the place,
and doing anything within its limits to so much as
muss Chandler's hair was probably a hanging offense.

He stood in the hall for about twenty minutes—
long enough for him to see the fan of light from
Chandler's door suddenly disappear. And only then
did he hie himself to Lily's door.

He rapped.

No answer.

She had a mad on, all right.

The door was locked, but he could deal with that if
necessary. Once again, he knocked softly and whispered, "Lil, honey?"

Still, no reply.

Well, he was damn sure going to get something
out of this evening! He dug in his pockets until he
found what he needed—a couple of short pieces of
stiff wire—and inserted them into the lock.

It wasn't hard to pick, but just as he felt the mech-
anism give way, the door magically opened.

There stood Lily, arms crossed, foot tapping, nose
in the air. "Have you taken up hotel burglary since we
last met?" she hissed.

She was pissed, all right. Slocum smiled. "No, just stealing the patrons from their rooms."

He pulled her out into the hall, picked her up, and carried her down to his room. She struggled, but not too hard. She fought him, but he noticed that she did so in quiet whispers and hisses.

And when he unlocked his door and pushed her into his room, she said, "Oh, you're maddening! I just hate you sometimes, Slocum!"

And then she threw herself into his arms.

He kissed her, kissed her hard, and at the same time used the arm that wasn't holding her to him to raise her flimsy gown's hem, gathering it into his fist like so much gossamer.

And when it was hiked up high enough, he let it fall—but not before he slid his hand to her fanny. The fabric fell down over his fingers, and he squeezed her bare backside.

She wiggled against him and deepened her kiss before she broke it off long enough to say, "Slocum honey, the bed?"

He kept on kissing her while he backed them up toward the waiting mattress, and when they got there, he pulled her down atop him. She straddled him and sat up long enough to pull the nightdress—he thought it was blue, although he had to admit he was more interested in what was under it—over her head and toss it to the floor.

She was as advertised and as he remembered. Her high, round, pink-nippled breasts fit into his hands and spilled over. Her waist was tiny, her hips full, and her legs were long and strong.

Of course, he couldn't see much of them at the moment. She had already released his aching cock and was bent over, laving the tip with her tongue.

"Have mercy, Lil," he whispered and pulled her to him.

She came willingly, and when he rolled her onto her back—and rolled on top of her—she already had her legs spread.

With one hand he shoved his britches down and out of the way while he toyed with one breast, then with the other. She was a miracle, his Lil. No wonder he couldn't stay away.

The tip of his shaft nudged at her moist opening, and she was so wet that he slipped in easily. She let out a long sigh, as if beyond contentment.

Propping himself on his elbows, he kissed her again and began to move inside her.

It didn't take her long. Before he had made a dozen thrusts, she arched her back, craned her neck back, and came with a huge clenching of her vaginal muscles and a cry. Which he had the sense to cover with his hand, even though that sudden internal squeeze pushed him over the edge, too.

A moment later, when they had both caught their breaths and could both talk again, she said, "Slocum? You're a beast."

He kissed her temple, then grinned at her. "I know it."

She frowned prettily. "Men. You're all the cock of the walk, aren't you?"

"Can't speak for anybody but myself, darlin'," he said as he moved to reach for the nightstand.

She watched his hand and grinned. "You bought champagne!"

He pulled it from its bucket, where it had been chilling in precious ice that had cost him more than the bubbly. The bartender said they brought it down from the mountains once a month. He'd been lucky to get it at all, since once it got to Poleaxe, he'd been told, it didn't last more than two days, even wrapped in cheesecloth, stuck in a Chicago cooler box, and kept in the root cellar.

He popped the cork. "For you, Lil, anything," he said as he poured out two glasses.

"Then get out of those clothes," she said as she took her glass. "But first, a toast."

"What to, this time?" he asked.

She pursed her lips for a second, then said, "Living the good life!"

Considering the source, Slocum figured that the phrase could have meant just about anything, but he clinked his glass against hers and downed it straightaway.

It wasn't the best champagne he'd ever had, but any champagne was better than none.

While Lil finished her glass, he managed to get his boots kicked off, his shirt and britches and gun belt off, then poured them each a second glass.

Lily, as naked as the day she was born and flushed from the champagne as well as their frenzied lovemaking, leaned back against the pillows.

Christ, she was beautiful!

He already felt a fresh stirring in his loins, and now he had no way to hide it.

Lily looked at his crotch. "My goodness, Slocum," she said with raised brows. "I'm shocked."

"I can't imagine anything shockin' you, Lily darlin'," he said. "Except maybe a man who didn't tumble for you."

She grinned. "Flatterer."

He grinned back. "Drink your champagne, wench."

"You going to ravish me again?"

"Wouldn't be surprised. Wouldn't be surprised if I just kept on ravishin' you till sunup."

She lay a hand across her throat. "Whatever will I do?"

Slocum chuckled. "Oh," he said, "you'll think of somethin', honey. You always do."

She brightened. "I do, don't I?"

Slocum had drained his glass by this time and set it aside. He'd just remembered about·Chandler being Felix Hamilton, and about old Red Eye's murder at Hamiton's hands. Lil had the most cussed way of distracting a fellow!

He said, "There's somethin' we need to talk about, Lil."

She put her glass down as well. "Oh, Slocum, I

think there's something we need to do first." She leaned toward him and took his member in her hand.

It seemed the damned thing had a mind of its own, because he was suddenly fully erect again.

"Aw, hell," he muttered as he pulled her atop him—and right down on his ready cock. "I forgot what it was, anyway."

Smiling wickedly, she wiggled her hips.

6

Charlie rose before the dawn.

He wasn't particularly well rested after his night of tossing and turning, and it took him all of two whole hours to finally get himself het up enough to grab a stray hand, put him in charge for the day, then strap on his gun belt and saddle his horse.

He was headed for town. He didn't exactly know what he'd do once he got there, but he'd decided that he'd go loco if he had to wait out there on that ranch anymore. It was just too much worry, wondering if some little piece of cheap Christmas trash was going to be leading the boss around by his balls.

In fact, he didn't know who to resent more: David Chandler for buying his ranch and then taking mercy on him and giving him a job, or that strumpet he'd got himself crazy over.

In fact, in Charlie's mind, this Tiger Lil girl was beginning to take on the facial characteristics and the mannerisms of the little whore Charlie had married himself.

God, he sure hoped to hell that she was dead! He'd aimed to make her that way, anyhow.

He hoped she'd died in misery and pain and that it

had lingered a long time, too, and that just before she gave her last gasp, she'd whispered, "I'm sorry, Charlie."

Not that he would have forgiven her, even then.

Women! he thought with a snort so loud that it startled his horse. Women and girls! If he'd had a daughter, he would have drowned her at birth, just to save some other poor bastard the trouble of killing her later on.

The pretty ones all grew up to be whores, gold diggers, painted hussies—or all three. The ugly ones all turned to Jesus and beat you over the head with a Bible the whole day and night long.

One way or the other, he was going to take care of this damnable business of Tiger Lil.

Although he'd been up since four, Miles Kiefer, Poleaxe's sheriff, showed up at the jail at eight o'clock in the morning, as usual.

He woke up the night deputy, Josh Childers, by swatting him with his hat. Josh's boots hit the floor with a bang—as usual—and he said, "Wasn't sleepin', Sheriff."

Also as usual.

Kiefer slipped a cup of lukewarm coffee under his nose, watched him take a sip, then wrinkle his nose. Josh was a good boy, but he still had some growing up to do.

"Keep tellin' you, Josh. Don't fall asleep. And don't let the coffee get cold."

"Yeah, yeah," Josh said and rubbed at his eyes, then his cheeks. "Sorry, Miles."

During this conversation, Sheriff Miles Kiefer had stoked up the stove again and set a fresh pot of coffee on to brew. Not only was Josh's pot too cool to drink, it probably had tasted like weak tea mixed with horse shit to begin with. He'd have to have a talk with the boy about that.

But not today. Something else was pressing closer to the top of his mind.

"Chair?" he said.

Remembering himself, Josh scrambled to his feet and vacated the chair in back of the desk. "Sorry," he said and started for the door. "See you tonight."

"Hold it just a minute, kid," Miles said and indicated that his deputy should have a seat opposite him. Josh did, although he looked puzzled.

"What is it?"

"I believe we've got us some trouble in town, that's all. May turn out to be nothing," Miles said, "but then again, you never can tell."

Josh leaned forward eagerly, his chin floating above the desk. He was still young enough, Miles supposed, that trouble sounded like fun. Well, he'd get over that. At least Miles hoped he would.

"You ever heard of a gunslinger named Slocum?" he asked.

If Josh had been a dog, his ears would have suddenly pricked to attention. "As in *the* Slocum? The famous shootist? The one in the dime books?"

Miles sighed. "That's the one." He'd been around over fifty years, and he knew better than to believe everything he read.

Especially those stupid dime books.

"You mean he's real?" Josh went on, and by the look of him, he could barely contain his excitement. "Is he the trouble?"

"Yes, and yes," replied Miles. "Well, maybe on that last yes. Might be he's here just mindin' his own business. For now, that's the attitude this office is going to take. But I just thought you should have a heads-up."

"He's really real?" Josh repeated. Miles wondered if the kid had heard anything else he'd said.

Again, Miles heaved a sigh. "Yes. Really. Don't believe those dime books, Josh. They're way off the mark about nine-tenths of the time."

But Josh wasn't listening. He was staring out the front windows. "Golly!" he muttered under his breath. "Slocum. In Poleaxe!"

"Josh?" Miles said. And when the kid didn't turn toward him, he said it again, only louder.

Josh appeared to come down to earth again, and his neck got a little red. "Sorry, Sheriff," he said and had the decency to look a tad flustered.

"Go home and get yourself some sleep," Miles said. "But don't let your mouth get the better of you. Understand me?"

Josh nodded but anxiously asked, "How'd you

know he was in town? What name's he travelin' under? Is he doing somethin' suspicious?"

"Stayin' at the hotel under the name of Slocum," Miles said with a small smile and a shake of his head. "And I saw him in the saloon last night. Came for Tiger Lil's second show and left halfway through."

"Well, that's suspicious right there!" the deputy almost shouted. "How could anybody leave when she's singin'?"

Miles shrugged. "Well, I did. Followed him over to the hotel."

"And?" Josh said eagerly.

"And I already told you. He's registered."

The deputy sat back in his chair, apparently disappointed.

"Don't get all soft on me, kid," Miles said, and stood up to check the coffee. It was starting to smell pretty decent. "Cheer up. He may do somethin' devious yet."

Josh brightened considerably.

After Josh took his leave and Miles was alone with his coffee, he spent a long time staring at the walls.

Slocum had come to town, and there might be a whole lot more trouble than he'd let on to Josh.

Oh, he already knew about the other crook in town: Chandler. He'd known from the start. But he'd thought it was wiser to close his eyes to it than end up shot, and thus, he'd kept his mouth closed.

And as it had turned out, Chandler was a regular pillar of society. At least, so far.

Miles had forgiven himself just a little bit for being a coward, for letting it go on for these past two years, but he hadn't found peace yet. It still bothered him. He still kept his finger—invisibly, of course—on everything Chandler was up to.

Of course, even if he did turn up anything shady, he didn't exactly know what he'd do about it.

He shrugged. "Probably nothing," he said aloud. "You blamed coward."

But now Slocum had come into town. He knew Slocum by sight and by reputation, although he hadn't met the man personally. He did know that Slocum was one tough hombre and not too picky about which side of the law he worked for.

Maybe Slocum was on to Chandler, too. He'd been watching Chandler last night, in between bouts of eyeballing Tiger Lil. Slocum hadn't caught sight of him, not that it would have mattered.

Slocum wouldn't have remembered him, anyhow. He wouldn't have remembered one fellow out of a crowd of dozens who had witnessed Slocum's gunfight with Wes Harper at El Diablo.

Miles shook his head. Now *that* was the stuff of dime novels, if you asked him. The face-off on Main Street at high noon, the scattering of bodies off the sidewalks like flies off a porch screen, the two opponents facing one another—and then Harper had drawn.

But Slocum proved faster. Harper had dropped to his knees, then his face, before he'd had a chance to fully clear leather.

Slocum had done the town of El Diablo a favor that day, but Miles didn't think it was for that reason that he'd gone up against Wes Harper. It had been something private. And right after, he just rode out of town, leaving the body in the street like so much trash.

Which, Miles had to admit, Harper had been.

But it still struck him as odd.

Well, there was nothing he could do about it then. And right now, there was nothing he could do about either Chandler or Slocum.

He sighed and reached down to open his bottom drawer. He pulled out a bottle of whiskey, poured about a jigger into his coffee, then put the bottle away. It was a little early in the morning, but what the hell.

If this wasn't a good excuse to have a belt, he didn't know what was.

Lil, too, was awake, although Slocum was still dead to the world. She slipped out from under his arm, brushed a kiss over his lips, and slid into her negligee again.

Peeking out into the hall and finding it clear of human traffic, she tiptoed down to her room and immediately washed herself as best she could with the water in the dresser's pitcher and bowl. God forbid that David should come knocking and find her smelling of another man.

The water basin did a pretty fair job, but she thought that a complete soak would do a much better one. Clutching her negligee tightly around her, she went out, climbed downstairs as far as the landing, and called, "Walt?"

He craned his head up toward her and appeared surprised to see her in such a state of barely dressed, but he gulped and asked, "Miss Lil?"

"I'd like to order a bath, please," she said and smiled. "Now, if possible."

He smiled back. They always did. He said, "Yes, ma'am. Right away, ma'am!"

She shrank back around the landing like a turtle pulling into its shell and walked back up to the top of the stairs—and saw David, big as life, standing outside her door.

"Good morning!" she chirped as she walked toward him, and tried to look as cheery as possible. "What are you doing up so early?"

He smiled, but he said, "I might ask you the same question."

She knew she didn't look rested. Who would, after making love until just before the dawn? So she said, "Oh, I just could barely sleep, David. I tossed and turned all night."

She reached him, gave him a chaste peck on the cheek, and opened her door, exposing a bed she already knew was in disarray. She'd been pretty mad at Slocum last night. That was, until he turned up.

He noted the mussed bed, she saw. "I was just

thinking too much, I guess," she added softly, with a little smile.

His face, which had been tight before, now relaxed. "Yes," he said. "I suppose you did have a lot to think over."

She nodded. "I just asked for a bath to be brought up." She thought she'd best throw that in. He would have got to wondering why she was at the other end of the hall in a nightdress.

"Ah," he said. "Well, I'll let you get to it then. I don't supposed you'd be in the mood for breakfast? I was going to ask you to go now, but later, perhaps?"

"That would be lovely, David," she purred.

He bent to kiss her, but she backed away while waggling her finger. "Now, now. This isn't the time or the place. Why, I'm barely dressed!"

He winked at her. "As if I hadn't noticed!"

Feigning embarrassment, she took another step away. "Go on with you, you rogue," she teased.

Doffing his hat, he bowed. "As you wish, m'lady."

He backed up to the center of the hall at the exact moment the first boy came, bearing a bucket of hot water, and nearly collided with him. Gracefully, he stepped aside, and the boy entered Lil's room. He eyed her, then opened his mouth to ask a question.

"Behind the screen," she said before he had a chance to ask.

"Two hours?" David asked.

"I'll meet you downstairs," she said.

He left at last, and Lily sank down upon her rumpled sheets. Thank God she'd thought to wash herself, as best she could, right away! And thank God she'd had the sense to only get near him once, to give him that hasty peck on the cheek.

All she needed was for him to be the least bit suspicious, especially today.

A second lad appeared with another bucket and passed the first, who hiked his thumb back toward the screen. The second boy eyed her but proceeded to the tub without a word.

David was a nice man, she thought. She was almost feeling guilty for planning to bilk him—but not guilty enough to call a halt to it. She'd worked too hard.

But then there was Slocum. Ah, Slocum, with his magic hands . . .

David could never be half the man in bed that Slocum was. David could never be half the man that Slocum was, period.

But David sure had a lot more money . . .

7

When Slocum woke, Lil was gone.

It didn't come as much of a surprise to him. He rolled over onto his back, worked the kink out of his neck, and sat up.

After he dressed, he ambled down to the hotel's restaurant to find some breakfast. He sat at a table in the back, and when the waiter came, he ordered a whopper of a breakfast: a sixteen-ounce steak (rare), six eggs (over easy), hash browns, a plate of toast, and a pot of strawberry preserves.

About the time his breakfast arrived, he noticed the young man in the corner. He was trying not to look Slocum's way—or at least, not get caught looking—but couldn't seem to help himself.

Slocum busied himself with his steak, all the while keeping an eye on the kid, if only with his peripheral vision. The boy's face didn't ring any bells with him. He could have been anybody. He was skinny and sandy-headed and clean-shaven. Looked to be a nice, clean-cut boy.

Until the boy turned to answer a question the waiter asked him, and the blouse-over where his shirt was tucked in lifted, and Slocum saw the side of a gun belt.

Still, it set off no alarms. This was the West. Just about everybody carried a hip gun.

Thoughtfully, Slocum slathered strawberry jam on a piece of toast. He didn't need some kid playing peek a boo this morning. He'd got so peach orchard crazy for Lil last night that he'd forgot about Chandler, and he intended to tell Lil today. He needed to do it.

Not that he thought Chandler meant Lil any harm right now. But when he finally figured out what she was up to, he'd probably revert to his old rotten self pretty damned quick.

Slocum didn't want to be around for that.

He didn't want Lil to be around for it, either.

Slocum sighed. What the hell did that damned kid want?

He was getting up now. And heading straight for Slocum's table.

And now that Slocum saw him head-on, he realized the kid wore a badge.

Great. Just great.

Well, he hadn't broken any laws. Yet. He swallowed his mouthful of toast and jam, took a sip of coffee, and pretended to be surprised when the kid stopped at his table.

"Morning, Mr. Slocum," said the boy, who, by his badge, was a deputy. His voice broke when he said "Slocum."

Slocum held back a smile. He looked up and said, "Mornin', Deputy. You have me at a disadvantage."

The boy looked surprised. He also looked like a confirmed dime book addict.

Slocum added, "You know my name, but I don't know yours."

The boy seemed relieved, but only a little. "My name's Deputy Josh Childers, Mr. Slocum, and I just wanted to . . ."

Slocum waved a fork. "Sit down, Deputy Josh."

This, too, seemed to surprise the deputy. But he said, "No, sir. I mean, thank you, but no. I just thought you oughta know that me and the sheriff know you're in town, that's all."

Slocum nodded. "Real observant, considering that I never tried to hide it."

The sarcasm was lost on Deputy Josh, who said, "Just thought you should know we're watchin' you. You'd best not go stirrin' up any trouble."

After a pause, Slocum asked, "You done talkin'?"

"Yeah, I reckon so."

"Then scat, Deputy, and let a man eat his breakfast in peace."

Deputy Josh stood there another moment, as if he was stuck between shooting Slocum and asking for his autograph. And then he suddenly turned on his heel and stomped out.

Slocum shook his head slowly. As he cut off another bite of steak, he muttered, "Decisions, decisions. Good thing you made the right one, Deputy."

For now, at least, he thought. He popped the steak into his mouth and began to chew.

* * *

At about a quarter to ten, Charlie rode up to the edge
of town. And stopped there, sitting in his saddle un-
easily. He'd come here full of intent, but as he'd
ridden—slower and slower, finally slowing to a
plod—the reality of what he was about to do hit
home. Or rather, the reality of exactly what he
should do.

And who would see him do it, whatever it was.

He sat back, the saddle creaking under his slight
weight, and pushed his hat back a couple of notches.

Would he be better off to plug Chandler or that
songbird bitch? Maybe he shouldn't shoot either one
of them. At least, not yet. After all, everybody in
town knew him.

He sure didn't want to hang for killing the likes of
either one of them.

On the other hand, he couldn't let some cheap,
spangled hussy come out and give him orders on his
own ranch, now, could he?

He might be able to live with his bitterness toward
Chandler for a while longer, at least, but the probabil-
ity of his moving a trollop out to the Circle C was too
much for Charlie to handle.

He couldn't bear it.

Neither could he bear the idea that he might possibly be hanging himself.

The town was in sight, but no more than that. He
got down off his horse right there in the middle of

the prairie, stood a moment, then sat down in the horse's shade. He took off his hat and gave a hard scratch to the back of his head before he slapped the hat back on.

He'd been too hotheaded, coming here like this. He had to have more of a plan, that was it. He had to think more than one step ahead.

Damn it, anyway!

And so he sat there thinking, his ass planted in the gravel amid the scrub, while he kept his eyes on the town and his horse grazed quietly.

Slocum sauntered down to the livery. He'd seen Chandler out on the street, so he'd taken a chance on Lily, but she'd shouted—from behind the closed door—that she was in the bathtub.

"Never bothered you before, having somebody to scrub your back," he said, smiling, his lips to the wood.

"Later, you handsome devil," she called back, and he'd complied.

When he got down to the livery, Jess—the old man who owned the place—was outside, staring off into the distance, transfixed. Now, this struck Slocum as a little odd. But then, he figured that everybody should have a hobby, no matter how addlepated or cracked in the head it looked to other folks.

So he strolled up to Jess—bald, dressed in overalls, and leaning on the pitchfork in his hand—and said, "Mornin'."

The stableman didn't look at him. "If you say so," he replied, his eyes on the distant prairie.

"How's my horse doin'?" Slocum asked, amused. He tried to remember if this was one of the men the barber had mentioned yesterday, and if he was daydreaming about Tiger Lil. No go, though. The barber had mentioned nearly the whole town, and he was damned if he could remember a quarter of the names.

If any of them.

"Fine," Jess replied. Obviously, he was one for few words. "I done like you said. Didn't turn him out with no other horses he could herd up. Grained him good. Bedded him deep."

"That's fine," Slocum replied, staring at the stableman's right ear, which happened to be the one toward him. "Thanks."

"No bother," said the man, still staring off into space.

Now, Panther was a fine horse, but he had roundup fever twenty-four hours a day, seven days a week. He'd leap fences to get at a gaggle of geese or a flock of sheep or a few head of cattle, just for the pleasure of bunching them up and making them stay put. He had other qualities that made up for this pain-in-the-ass quirk, though.

"Guess I'll go in and take a look at him," Slocum

said, and turned on his heel. "Maybe give him a good grooming."

But he'd gone no farther than two steps when the stableman asked, "What you suppose he's doin' out there, mister?"

Slocum turned around. "Who?"

The stableman raised his arm and pointed to a distant speck.

Slocum squinted. He finally made out the horse—a sorrel, he thought—which was tacked up and grazing. At first, he thought that maybe the horse had tossed his rider, then wandered off. But then he caught a speck of color down toward the ground.

A man, sitting.

The speck moved, apparently to scratch his head, because his hat moved along with his hand and arm.

"Strange," muttered Slocum.

"Been out there for near an hour, I reckon," the stableman said. "Least, that's how long I've had my eye on him."

"Must not be a whole lot to do in this town," Slocum said dryly.

"Aside from droolin' over Miss Tiger Lil Kirkland?" the man asked, still never taking his eyes away from the distant figure. "Nope. Not a whole helluva lot. And quit bein' sarcastic with me, son."

"Right." Shaking his head and chuckling, Slocum went into the stable to check on his horse.

Panther was fine, just fine—bedded down in a

roomy stall with the extra straw that Slocum had paid for, and munching good alfalfa hay. He flicked his ears toward Slocum, gave a snort of recognition, then turned his attention to the hay again.

Muttering, "I'm overjoyed to see you, too, horse," Slocum checked to make sure that his water bucket was full—it was—and that he had been grained. Which it looked like he had, since there were a few grains of oats on the aisle outside the stall, and Panther's feed trough was licked clean.

Slocum picked up a curry comb and a body brush, let himself into the stall, and went to work. There was nothing better for the inside of a man than the outside of a horse, his pappy used to say.

Of course, his pappy hadn't met Lil, but she wasn't handy at the moment.

By the time he'd finished brushing Panther, combing his mane and tail, and picking out his hooves, he was still the only human in the stable. Odd, he thought, that the stableman hadn't at least come in to check on his charges. Or Slocum.

He put a hand on the Appy's glistening neck. "See you later, Panther," he mumbled, and let himself out of the stall.

Sure enough, when he walked outside, that stableman was still in the same place, staring at the distant speck of a horse.

"You wanna chair or anything?" Slocum asked, half teasing.

"Maybe he got throwed out there," came the reply, although he didn't seem much concerned about it. "Maybe he can't get up."

Slocum pursed his lips. "Maybe not."

"Reckon somebody oughta take a ride out there and see if he's all right." It wasn't a question. It was more on the order of an observation, Slocum thought. Or a request.

But he fell for it.

Slocum said, "Why don't you ride on out?"

At least it'd take your mind off all these pressing matters you've got weighing down on you, he thought sarcastically.

Slowly, the stableman shook his head. "Nope. Got to see to business. Runnin' the livery and all."

Straight-faced, Slocum said, "Sure. I can see where that's a big responsibility. Keeps a man busy, on his toes, like."

At long last, the man turned his head to look Slocum in the eye. "Reckon you could take a ride out there, though. That is, if you ain't got nothin' better to do than sass an old man."

Slocum said nothing.

"Why, that poor feller might be all stove up," urged the stableman, then shook his head. "Poor feller. Might even be dyin'."

Slocum folded his arms. "Might be dead already. Might have died while you were standin' here, watchin' him."

•

The stableman shook his head and resumed staring into the distance. "Nope." He sounded a little disappointed. "He just moved a tad bit."

"Well, I'll watch your livery," Slocum offered, holding back a grin. It was getting more and more difficult to keep the laughter inside. "You go on. Ride out there and see what the trouble is."

"Like to," the old man said. "I'd purely love to. But I ain't got no horse'a my own."

Slocum knew when he was beat. He also knew what his threshold was for holding back what was building into a roar of laughter. He said, "All right. You win, old-timer. I'll go on out and have a look-see. Just wait till I get my horse saddled."

"Don't bother."

"What?"

"Don't bother to saddle up. Take my cousin Willie's nag. He's all ready to go. Just inside the door, there."

Slocum would have asked why, for the love of God, the livery owner hadn't just ridden out there on Cousin Willie's horse himself! But in the end, he simply grabbed Cousin Willie's horse and swung up.

Funny thing, though.

He hadn't ridden a quarter of the way to the far-off horse and his ground-sitting rider when the rider jumped up, mounted the horse, and took off in the opposite direction.

And at a dead gallop, at that.

Slocum reined Cousin Willie's horse to a halt and

just sat there for a second or two, watching the stranger's dusty trail dissipate in the light breeze.

Shaking his head slowly and chuckling to himself, he reined Cousin Willie's horse around and started back to the livery at a slow jog.

8

David Chandler sat in his rocker out front of the hotel, watching the little drama down the street. Just what the hell were those two idiots up to? Not that it mattered much. Jess, the livery owner, could be entertained by watching cactus grow, and the one with him—or rather, the one now riding back—was a stranger to him.

Nothing ever happened in Poleaxe. Nothing except Lily, he thought, smiling.

And then he wondered who the stranger was. Might be that Slocum, the one the clerk had mentioned to Lil. Beneath his breath, Chandler chuckled. These fellows who saw Lil sing onstage once, then convinced themselves they knew her!

Must be a pretty empty life. But then, he reminded himself, for most cowhands and saddle tramps, it *was* a pretty empty life, and a lonely one.

Chandler furrowed his brow. A fellow like that might turn out to be troublesome. A fellow like that might just have convinced himself that he and Lil had truly met, maybe even that she was in love with him. Was waiting for him, in fact.

But then he snorted and rocked back. "Idiot," he

muttered. He had been out of the action for far too long. He was turning shadows into monsters.

Still, something about this fellow's name . . .

Down at the end of the street, the stranger dismounted and handed the horse over to Jess. Chandler watched, rocking, and then quite suddenly, stopped stock-still. Slocum?

No, it couldn't be that fellow from the dime books. Could it? He'd never admit it out loud, but he'd read a few. Most of them were fictionalized. At least, the couple in which he, as Felix Hamilton, was mentioned were entirely fictional, that was for sure. He'd assumed the Slocum books were made up, too.

But this man seemed to fit the description.

Except, he thought with a tiny sigh of relief, that this particular man named Slocum wasn't riding a flashy horse. What did he always ride in the dimers? A paint? No, an Appaloosa, that was it.

Well, that was a plain old bay he'd just gotten down from. It could have been any one of a couple dozen, right here in town.

A chuckle made its way through Chandler's lips once more. He was shadow boxing again, and he'd caught himself at it.

The Slocum walking up the street was nothing more than a conveniently named saddle tramp who'd seen Lil sing somewhere or other. He'd caused no trouble so far and likely wouldn't.

Dipping his fingers into a vest pocket, he pulled out his watch. Almost eleven.

He glanced upward, as if he could see through the porch roof and right into Lil's room. Damn! That was probably one pruned-up woman by now! Hell, he'd take her anyway, he thought as he slipped his pocket watch back in place.

He'd take her, and take her, and take her . . .

He fell into thought again—mostly about the wonder that was Lily. In fact, he lost track of time until, suddenly, someone jerked him right out of his chair and onto the sidewalk.

And he couldn't say whether he heard the gun report in the split second before, during, or after.

He scrambled for cover, right on the heels of the fellow who had jerked him aside. It wasn't until he dived down, off the sidewalk and around the corner of the building, that he got a look at his savior's face.

"You all right?" the man he'd supposed was Slocum asked him, although Slocum's eyes weren't on him. He was squinting out into the distance, his gun drawn.

"Fine," Chandler answered. This was certainly a turn of events! "And thank you, stranger."

Slowly, Slocum holstered his gun, gave a shake to his head, then finally turned toward Chandler. "Welcome," he said, then pointed to Chandler's temple. "You're bleedin' a mite. And the name's Slocum."

Chandler touched his head. He was bleeding. He pulled the white handkerchief from his pocket and held it to his temple.

Slocum stood up and held down his hand. "I

reckon he's gone." As he helped Chandler up he added, "Don't know what good I thought I'd manage with a handgun. Feller was out a good ways."

Chandler gained his feet and continued to dab at his head with the handkerchief as he followed Slocum back up onto the porch. People were poking their heads out of doors and windows like so many snails, timidly emerging from their shells.

From across the street, Bart Cummings hollered, "You all right, Mr. Chandler?"

"Fine," Chandler called back.

Sheriff Kiefer was trotting down the street, straight for him, waving. "You hurt?" he called. "What the Sam Hill happened?"

Chandler shook his head, both to indicate that he was fine, and that he had no idea. Who the hell would shoot at him? At least, who from Poleaxe? He'd made a point of staying on his best behavior from the second he'd come into town.

Slocum, he noticed, was fiddling with the wall, right where he'd been sitting. The man, better than six feet of him stood up just as the sheriff arrived. Slocum said, "If that slug didn't crease your skull, must'a been a splinter. You know anybody who's—"

"Slocum," Sheriff Kiefer said. Chandler noticed that he didn't say it as a question. It was more as if he was labeling Slocum, in the same manner that he'd point to the ground and say, "Dirt."

* * *

Slocum turned to face the sheriff. "Seems you've got a sniper in your flock, Sheriff."

He'd said it calmly, although something about the way the man had said his name irritated the hell out of him.

The sheriff's brow furrowed. "Sniper?"

Slocum pointed out past the livery and the end of town. "Fella was out there earlier. I started out to him on account of your stableman thought he might be hurt."

"And?" the sheriff urged, although none too eagerly. Slocum could tell that he'd rather lock up the first handy stranger—well, the first handy stranger named Slocum, anyhow—and let it go at that.

"And he rode off, over the ridge. Shot came from out there. He must have snuck back, fired from that low ridge."

The sheriff shook his head slowly, as if in disbelief. "Do you know how far away that ridge is, Slocum?"

"'Bout two hundred and fifty yards, I reckon. And you know my name well enough to use it every five seconds, but I ain't had the pleasure of your acquaintance." Slocum had tried to keep his cool, but his words came out with a grain of irritation anyway.

The sheriff frowned at him. "Sheriff Kiefer's good enough."

"Gentlemen, gentlemen!" Chandler took each of them by a shoulder. "What's all this hostility? Miles, this gentleman saved my life by yanking me out of my rocker in the nick of time. I very much doubt that he could have been on this porch and clear out there at the same time! If, indeed, that's what you're accusing him of."

Slocum couldn't decide whether to hate Chandler or like him. Or feel sorry for him, because of Lil. At the moment, he carried all three sentiments.

"If you say so, Mr. Chandler," the sheriff growled, but he was looking at Slocum. "Slocum, I got my eye on you. Remember that."

Slocum didn't reply, and the sheriff turned on his heel, headed back up the street toward his office.

"Don't seem too eager to get after the culprit, does he?" Slocum said.

"Must figure whoever it was is long gone by this time," Chandler said.

Neither man looked at the other. They were both watching the sheriff's retreating back.

Upstairs on the second-floor porch, Lil listened. Fresh from her bath, she was wrapped in a negligee, had a towel wrapped around her head and another absently clutched to her throat. She had come running when she heard the ruckus, for there was no one more basically nosy than Lily Kirkland.

It was a trait that served her well in her line of work.

What were Slocum and David doing down there, anyway? Was it possible that they might be—God

forbid—bonding? Every time she thought she understood men, the species came up with something new
to flummox her.

She, too, watched the sheriff walk up the street
and enter the jail, and then she heard David speak
again.

"Buy you a drink?" he asked. "Least I can do for a
man who saved my life."

And just as she thought, *Don't do it, Slocum,* he
spoke.

"Sure," Slocum said. "Be obliged."

With a stomp of her foot, Lil turned on her heel
and marched back to her room.

Behind green velvet drapes, Chandler had a private
table reserved. After all, it was his saloon. At least,
that's what Slocum figured, although it was a different place than Chandler had perched himself when
Lil was onstage. That had been right up front, while
this one was in a corner on a little wood-railed plat-
form a step higher than the rest of the floor.

The barkeep brought them a couple of glasses and
a bottle of what Slocum recognized as excellent
bourbon. As the bartender poured, Chandler reached
into his pocket. He held out what looked like a ma-
hogany cigar case, delicately inlaid with silver.

"Smoke?" he asked.

"Don't mind if I do," Slocum said as he reached
for one. All this largesse was appreciated, but Slocum
wasn't going to judge the man on whiskey and cigars.

He was Lil's unwitting target, after all, which would tend to create a little sympathy with anyone. Then again, he was, in a way, Slocum's rival.

Plus which, he had killed old Red Eye. Couldn't forget that.

It wasn't that Slocum had any claims on Tiger Lil, but still . . .

But there was something else about the man—aside from the aforementioned list of sins—that just scraped Slocum the wrong way. He couldn't put a label on it, didn't know what it was. Just *something*.

The bartender walked away, his job finished, and Chandler picked up his shot glass. Slocum followed suit.

"To Slocum, the man who saved my life," Chandler said.

"I'll drink to that," Slocum replied before he upturned his shot glass. It was the good stuff, all right. "Smooth," he said. "Obliged."

Chandler picked up the bottle and poured them each another shot. He toyed with his glass for a moment, then asked, "You're him, aren't you? The Slocum in the dime books, I mean."

Slocum didn't reply.

"Sheriff Kiefer is usually an easy sort to get along with," Chandler continued. "He seemed to know you right off. And as I recall, you said you'd never met him."

"True on all accounts," Slocum admitted. "Although those dime books are full of shit, and I have kind of a hard time believin' that Kiefer's an easy-goin' sort. But I'll take your word for it." He took a sip of his whiskey. It was too good to gulp a second time.

Chandler laughed.

Back up at the jail, Miles Kiefer was busily going through his filing cabinets, searching for something—anything—that would give him legal cause for running Slocum out of town.

Or locking him up.

He hadn't been pleased about Slocum being in town in the first place, and he especially wasn't happy about what he saw as a budding friendship between Slocum and Chandler. If those two got together, who the hell knew what sort of goings-on might transpire?

He liked his town quiet. He was willing to let Chandler go about his business, so long as he kept his nose clean. But this new situation made him as itchy as hell.

He supposed he could have ordered Slocum out of the city limits, just on his say-so. Local sheriffs pulled similar stunts all the time. After all, they were pretty much the only law in their towns, unless the U.S. Marshal's Office got involved.

But Kiefer wouldn't put it past Slocum to have some crooked contacts with high-ranking badges—the sort that could boot a local sheriff out of his job and get him blackballed all over the West. It wasn't a very pleasant thought.

He didn't have too high an opinion of Slocum. Not much better than his opinion of Chandler.

He wished that he could just bag them up in the middle of the night and drown them like a couple of kittens. But that was out of the question.

First of all, it would be against his personal moral code, not to mention the law. And second, they were too big.

He snorted under his breath, and opened another file drawer. Maybe he'd find something in this one. . . .

9

Charlie Townsend didn't stop his galloping horse until he was almost a fourth of the way home and was absolutely certain there was no one on his tail. He reined his lathered mount up a low, rocky rise and into a clump of trees and sat for a long time, watching and waiting.

But no one came. Not even after he had cooled down his horse, waited a whole hour, and eaten the beef sandwich he'd packed, just in case.

They must not have spotted him, that was all he could figure. He'd fired and run, simple as that. Hadn't even waited to see if his shot hit home or not. Charlie had been a crack sniper during the war—he'd even been an instructor—but he was getting on, now.

Still, even at his advanced age, he was pretty sure he'd hit what he was aiming at.

He supposed the smart thing to do would be to ride on back to the ranch and wait for somebody to bring them the sad news. No more Mr. High-and-Mighty David Chandler, no more Mrs. Future Tiger Lil Slut-Whore Chandler . . .

Maybe he could talk some of the boys into going

in with him and buying the ranch. He hadn't thought about that possibility before.

In fact, he hadn't really thought about the aftermath at all, he realized belatedly. He'd only thought about Chandler bringing that woman out to the ranch.

He checked his horse's cinch, was satisfied, and swung up. He'd figure something out, he thought. Too late now to do anything else.

He hadn't wasted much time at all on worrying about that fellow that rode at him, from down at the livery back in town.

He didn't waste any more on it now.

He set off for the ranch at a lazy lope and tried to figure out how to best handle getting hold of the ranch again—or at least, part of it—and on how he should react when the sheriff came to bring the sorry news of Chandler's death.

Chandler and Slocum were getting pretty sozzled. Chandler had drunkenly called for another bottle of his fancy hooch, and Slocum was happy to help him drink it.

Slocum, however, wasn't as well-oiled as Chandler thought he was, or as Chandler was himself. He seemed to have completely forgotten his near miss with death and was regaling Slocum with stories from his past.

Slocum knew there was something wrong with them. Of course, a drunken man is apt to forget details, or overemphasize them, or confuse them with those from other stories or events. But even to Slocum's partially muzzy mind, Chandler was just plain making things up—or leaving out pertinent details.

Besides, he thought as he sipped at his bourbon, Red Eye O'Neill hadn't been anywhere near the Dakotas in '73. He'd been down in the border country, fighting Indians with Slocum.

"Yeah, you should'a known ol' Red Eye," Chandler said wistfully. His speech was getting sloppier by the moment. Slocum expected him to fall headfirst onto the table at any moment.

"Guess so," Slocum replied. He hadn't admitted knowing anybody, not even his pappy. Not to this man. There was something really wrong about him.

Just exactly what was it? That was up for grabs, although Slocum had a hunch that maybe he'd been wanted at one time or another. It was the way he talked about the dime books, but it was more the stuff he left out of his stories, the substitutions he made in their characters.

He actually began to worry more about Lil than her mark.

Now, that was something new.

He tried to steer the conversation—which was turning into an oratory about another of Chandler's adventures up along the Pecos, a place that, by the way he described it, Slocum automatically knew Chandler had never been—back to the point.

" 'Scuse me, Chandler," he said, interrupting the

man's sentence, but just who the hell do you think was shootin' at you?"

Chandler just shrugged and poured himself another shot.

"I mean, it musta been somebody you know. And it musta been a sniper. I mean, a professional. A man don't fire from that far out and miss a feller by inches if he wasn't tryin' to kill him."

Chandler shrugged. "Mayhap he was aimin' at something else." And then, one brow hiked, he stared at Slocum. "You, maybe?"

Slocum thought he'd said that just a little too hopefully, but he twirled his shot glass, making damp circles on the polished wood, and said, "Hell, if that feller was tryin' to kill me, I'd'a made a helluva lot better target when I was down to the livery." He took another sip to drain the glass, and thoughtfully added, "Better yet when I was ridin' out there to see who it was."

Chandler appeared disappointed. "Oh, yeah . . . forgot."

Suddenly, the bartender appeared beside their table. Chandler looked up with a start. "Christ, man, don't creep up like that!"

The barkeep didn't flinch. It was apparent this wasn't the first time he'd seen his boss drunk, and it wasn't the first time Chandler had yelled at him, either. He asked, "Just wanted to see if you gents were in the mood for some lunch. We got some nice roast beef and fried chicken, and—"

"Go away!" Chandler roared.

But Slocum reached out and caught the retreating bartender's arm. "You got bread and mustard to go with that beef?" he asked.

"Yessir, fresh baked this morning."

"I'll take a nice thick beef sandwich, then. And a beer to go with it." He turned back to Chandler. "Hate to call an end to drinkin' this good whiskey, but I'd best get some rib-stickin' food into me, or I'll pass out before nightfall!"

Chandler seemed to consider this for a moment before he yelled across the bar, "Hey you!" He appeared to have forgotten the bartender's name. "I'll have the same!"

"Yessir, Mr. Chandler," came the muted reply.

"Better damned well be 'yessir,'" Chandler muttered, barely loud enough for Slocum to hear.

But he did hear it, and he made a mental note.

Tiger Lil, bathed and dressed and ready for the day in a deep purple silk dress, sashayed downstairs at roughly noon. She expected to find David Chandler waiting on the porch and was surprised when he wasn't there. The desk clerk appeared from somewhere—possibly the saloon, because she couldn't imagine him straying any farther from his post—stepped up on the porch, and tipped his hat.

"Afternoon, Miss Lil," he said amiably. "Bet you're looking for Mr. Chandler."

"As a matter of fact, Walt, I—" she began before he broke in.

"He's over to the saloon, drinking with that fella who rode in yesterday," he said. "The one who said he knew you?"

Lil gave her brow an indifferent hike. "If you knew how many times I've heard that . . ." she said, and then was drowned out by the clatter of the stage-coach rumbling and banging its way past her en route to the depot.

She pulled out a hankie and made a show of dust-ing her bodice and dabbing at her face. "Beastly things," she said as she watched the coach draw to a halt before its destination: the Butterfield office.

It was probably packed full of people come to town to see her, she realized. At least, it had been every day so far. They'd had to put on an extra stage each day, just to accommodate her loyal fans.

Such as they were.

"Sorry, ma'am," the desk clerk said automatically, as if he should have controlled the stagecoach, but couldn't. She could tell he was as besotted with her as the rest of the town.

She smiled at him rather kindly and said, "Oh, my! It's not your fault, dear."

At that "dear," the man nearly keeled over. Well, she thought, he wobbled a little. She added, "I don't mean to keep you from your work, then."

She made a classy exit, she thought, and walked up the sidewalk, toward the saloon.

* * *

Up at the Butterfield depot, a man got off with five others. All six had shared the crowded conveyance for no other reason than to see and hear the famous Tiger Lil. The sixth, for one, was sick of listening to tales of her legendary beauty, her nightingale voice, and her fabled charm.

Bill Messenger stepped away from the others, who milled on the sidewalk, and brushed the stink of travel and too many unwashed bodies off his clothes.

Or tried to.

He didn't have much success. Finally, he picked up his carpetbag and left his companions without a word or a backward glance. He didn't know them. A bunch of dirt farmers come to gawk, that's what they were.

Oh, he hadn't said a word, but he was here to see Tiger Lil, too, but for a very different reason.

He was going to kill her.

He walked down the center of the dusty street, taking in the town, taking in the poster of her in front of the saloon with a single, disapproving grunt, and made his way into the hotel.

"May I help you?" the clerk asked.

"Need a room," Messenger said flatly. "For two days, no more."

"Very good, sir," the clerk said, and swiveled the book toward him so that he could sign it. "That'll be fifty cents a day, in advance, if you don't mind. Bath's another fifty, or you can get one down to the barbershop for a quarter. You just come in on the stage?"

"Yeah," said Messenger as he signed the ledger. John Smith. He dug into his pocket and pulled out a half buck in change, and added, "Believe I'll head down to the barbershop. And it'll be just the one day."

The clerk quickly eyed the ledger and said, "Yessir, Mr. Smith. That'll be number fourteen, when you get back. Nice view of the main street."

Messenger nodded. "Thanks."

As he headed back for the door, the clerk called, "Dining room's right here." He pointed toward the wide pocket doors and the large room beyond. "And next door's the saloon. You're in for a treat, if you like singing, or just looking. We've got Miss Tiger Lil Kirkland performing two shows a night. The one and only Tiger Lil, herself!"

Messenger hesitated and turned his head from the dining room doors, back toward the clerk. "Saw the sign," he said flatly and walked out the door.

He headed down the street to the barbershop. Three years back, Lil had taken him for every cent he was worth, but he still had the feeling that she shouldn't be shot by a grimy man. Didn't seem right somehow, no matter how low she'd turned out to be.

No, a man should be clean all over and shaved when he killed her.

It just seemed fitting.

*   *   *

Lil stood inside the batwing doors of the Poleaxe Saloon, her arms crossed, her head slowly shaking as she looked across the expanse at David Chandler's private table.

There sat David and Slocum, drunker than two lords, trying to fight their way through two of the thickest roast beef sandwiches she'd ever seen. It wouldn't be too swift an idea to let them know she was there, she figured. In their condition, who knew what they were apt to say? Or what Slocum might let slip!

Besides, the whole thing ticked her off. They weren't supposed to be palling around like this!

David was supposed to be pining away while he waited for her answer, and Slocum was supposed to be drooling over her, in absentia.

Humph!

Luckily, besides the two men and the barkeep, the place was deserted, and she slipped back out onto the walk undiscovered. She huffed a little sigh again, at the same time shrugging her shoulders, and turned back toward the hotel.

But only turned, because she was immediately caught up in what seemed a sea of men: groveling men, scraping and bowing men.

Now, this was more like it!

"Hello, boys," she said with a broad, inviting smile.

One man managed to croak out, "M-m-miss Lil!"

If Chandler was too drunk to take her for one of those damned buggy rides and plead for her hand until she wanted to slug him, and Slocum was too sozzled to show her any fun in the bedroom, well then, she'd just have to make her own fun, wouldn't she?

And there was nothing she liked better than a pack of fawning men.

"I was just going up to the hotel dining room to have my midday repast," she said rather grandly, and began to stroll.

They followed along like a swarm of gnats, as she knew they would: buzzing and flitting and tripping over their words—and feet.

She found it amusing. And also comforting, in a way.

She stopped walking, and so did they. "Would you gentlemen care to join me?" she asked with a finger to her chin—and just the right amount of naïveté. "I'll bet you fellows just got off that stage, and also I'll bet you're as hungry as a bunch of billy goats."

This actual invitation—even though that billy goat remark had been vaguely insulting—set them into an even greater flurry of excitement. She counted heads. There were five of them, each one more awestruck and eager than the next. And each head was bare, for they all held their hats in their hands as they nodded, suddenly too shy to talk.

Well, hell. She might even spring for their meal. Farmers, by the look of them. They probably didn't have a hotel meal more often than every five years or so. If that.

If Slocum and David could get drunk on their butts in the middle of the day, she could, by God, play Lady Bountiful for one afternoon!

Besides, her ego could use a few strokes.

10

It was close to nightfall, and Charlie, who had been careful to fix up some fences before he came in with the other hands, paced the floor of the bunkhouse.

"All that walkin' ain't gonna cook it any faster," Cookie grumped from beside the iron stove. He was making beef stew—again—and he was just tossing in a bowl's worth of raw, sliced carrots.

"Yeah, yeah," Charlie said and pushed his way past Pete to go have another look down the road to town.

But it was empty. Stark, bare, empty.

He couldn't believe that nobody had come to tell them that their boss had been killed. Well, actually, he couldn't believe that he'd missed, that was the truth of it. But he must have, because there sure wasn't anybody coming from town.

Of course, he thought, mayhap Chandler wasn't dead. Yet. Maybe they didn't want to alarm the ranch unnecessarily.

But why the hell not? Charlie ground his teeth. He wasn't that bad a shot, was he?

He should have waited to see Chandler fall. He should have been made of sterner stuff. He had been, once, long ago, during the war.

He'd probably been a better shot then, too . . .

No! Hadn't he dropped that mountain lion with one shot just last year? It was nearly as far away from him as Chandler had been.

Well, maybe the cat had been a tad closer.

Still, it was beyond him that nobody had sent word that if Chandler wasn't dead, he was, at least, mortally wounded. What kind of a lousy, heartless town was Poleaxe, anyhow?

Ed Riley came out of the barn and headed toward him. Ed was a bull of a fellow, dark-haired and swarthy complected. His daddy might have been Irish, but his mama had been something else entirely.

"What you doin' out here, Charlie?" he asked.

Charlie remembered when everybody used to call him "Mr. Townsend." It still rankled, being one of the hired help.

But he didn't let on. He said, "Just killin' time. Cookie's still butcherin' the steer."

Ed laughed, a rough, deep sound. "Well, believe I'll go in anyway. I was whitewashin' the damn corral fences all morning and pitchin' hay all afternoon long, and I'm past tired."

Charlie grunted, and Ed walked away without further comment.

Once Ed was out of earshot, Charlie muttered, "That'll be about the last time you get to call me 'Charlie,' Ed."

He momentarily forgot that he didn't have the

wherewithal to buy back the Circle C. He momentarily forgot that he didn't own it already, just by the force of his having the guts to pull the trigger this afternoon. And for a moment, he was actually happy.

As happy as Charlie Townsend ever was, anyway.

It never lasted too long.

Bill Messenger ate his supper not at the hotel but down the street at a dingy little cubbyhole called Mandy's Kitchen. If the kitchen was as grubby as the dining room—or what they laughingly called the place were he, along with six strangers, sat at one long, scarred table—he'd rather not know about it.

He was cleaned and shaved, had gone down to the livery and checked it out for tomorrow night, just in case he was still in town, and had been in and out of his hotel room twice without catching sight of Lil.

Which as a good thing. Considering what he had in store for her, that was.

At least, that's what he told himself. Secretly, he was half afraid that she wouldn't even recognize him when she saw him. Sure, she'd bilked quite a few men in her day, but a fellow liked to think he was special.

He snorted, and the man next to him, a short, balding fellow in a suit that had seen better days, said, "Beg pardon, mister?"

"Nothin'," Bill Messenger mumbled, and looked away. "Didn't say nothin' at all." Sure, he'd be out of here before anybody knew what had happened, but it never paid to make a point of being seen, of standing out.

Especially in a little town where probably half the current population, if not more, had come to see Lil perform.

They didn't know the half of it. If they could have seen the continuing performance that Lil had put on with him, they would have cheered and whistled for a week straight. They'd have called her the greatest actress of the age.

She'd hustled him, plain and simple, and slick and slippery as a bucket full of eels. She'd spent a week in town—that was back up in Cheyenne—batting her eyelashes and promising him her hand, and everything that went along with it. And the next thing he knew, he was married and she was gone—along with everything he owned in this world.

And he'd been so ashamed of his damned stupidity, so humiliated to have fallen for her line, that he'd left town and tried to disappear.

But he only sank further and further into poverty and a whiskey bottle before he did something really stupid. Over in the Dakotas, close to the Black Hills, he'd tried to hold up a stagecoach.

Tried, that was the operative word. He'd been drunk as a lord at the time, and the stage driver had put a stop to his short-lived career as a highwayman— and nearly his life—with one bullet.

Well, he didn't limp anymore.

And he'd served his time in prison. Got six months knocked off for good behavior, too.

He'd stopped drinking, as well, stopped cold. That was the only good thing he could think of about prison, other than it gave a man time to mull things over, time to plot out his revenge; time to kick himself up one side and down the other for his mistakes.

That was, when he wasn't getting kicked around by the other inmates.

Or the guards.

When he'd gotten out, the first thing he'd done was to track down Lil. His wife.

Now, that was a laugh, wasn't it? She was probably already married to half the men in the West. The ones worth the taking, that was.

The waiter began bringing bowls out from the kitchen. They served family style at Mandy's Kitchen, and although he had his doubts about the sanitation, at least they served a lot.

Actually, the food was pretty good: big, heaping bowls of mashed potatoes and green beans with bacon; platters heaped with peppered pork chops; boats of pork gravy; plates of carrots and celery and sweet pickles and beets. But Messenger was so caught up in his thoughts, both of the past and what he was about to do, that he barely noticed.

He pushed back his chair when they finally brought out the dessert, and left the café while the other patrons descended on the cherry and apple pies like vultures.

He had a full evening ahead of him.

David Chandler, sobered by a big lunch and almost two pots of coffee, ran a brush over his hair one more time, tugged at his jacket, and fussed with his tie, even though it didn't need fussing with.

This was it. A truly momentous occasion.

Straightening his shoulders, he took a deep breath, then walked from his room, up the hall to Lil's, and rapped at the door.

He didn't know if he was more excited or terrified. In a few moments, he would know—with absolute certainty—what his future held.

The door opened slowly, and there was Lil, absolutely resplendent in a russet gown, its neckline cut low to reveal the deep shadow of her décolletage. Despite himself, he gulped like a boy.

Lil smiled and came out into the hall, out to him. "Hello, David, dear," she purred.

Inside, he went all to mush. On the outside, things were a little stiffer.

He offered his arm.

Smiling, she slipped hers through it and laid her little hand over his wrist.

He began, "Lil, my dearest—"

But she hushed him with a finger to his lips. "It's not quite six yet, David."

She was going to drag it out to the end, wasn't she? But he said, "Yes, my love. I can wait ten minutes longer."

He made a show of slipping the watch from his pocket, checking the time, and then said, "Eight and a half, to be precise."

She laughed and hugged his arm tighter, pressing her breasts against his arm, deepening the shadow of her cleavage. Now, that was a good sign, wasn't it?

Softly, she said, "I swan, David, you just slay me! Now take me down to dinner."

Down the street at Mandy's Kitchen, Slocum finally pushed back from the table. Chandler had finally opted for coffee to sober himself up, but Slocum found that a good meal usually did him better. He'd had three pork chops, a mountain of mashed potatoes, and he'd just polished off his third piece of pie.

Mandy, whoever she was, was a mighty fine cook and not a bit stingy with the portions.

The crowd at the table was a motley one, men in dusty suits, men who looked as if they'd just come in off the ranch, men slickered up for something— probably for Tiger Lil's performance—and one elderly woman who sat at the end of the table and would have nothing to do with the conversation.

Slocum had stayed silent, too. He been more intent on soaking up all that excellent whiskey with plenty of chuck. But he'd listened.

The dinner conversation had been about one thing, and one thing only: Lil. She was truly the biggest thing to hit this town in, well, forever.

In fact, the only one who wasn't going to see her show tonight—most with plans to stay for the second performance—was the old lady, who frowned disapprovingly every time Lil's name was mentioned.

Slocum hadn't said, but he was going, too. And there was one fellow, at the other end of the table, who hadn't said much of anything, including his plans for the night.

Now, that fellow was a tad interesting to Slocum. Not just because he didn't say much. Hell, Slocum never said much, either. But because he had an air about him that Slocum couldn't figure out.

The man was freshly shaved, and if he'd ridden into town today, he'd taken the trouble to knock most of the dust off his clothes. He was tallish, about an inch shorter than Slocum was, and had close-cropped, sandy brown hair and a similar mustache.

He ate with one arm wrapped protectively around his plate, in the manner of somebody who'd been in prison for a while, but he didn't have the face of a criminal. He looked like somebody who'd had money, maybe for a long time, and gotten to take it for granted.

But if he was eating at Mandy's Kitchen when the hotel dining room was just up the street, chances were that he didn't have it anymore.

Well, that was a mystery, all right, but it wasn't exactly the thing on Slocum's front burner.

Chandler had let it slip that tonight, at six o'clock, he was expecting Lil's answer to his proposal. Oh, Slocum knew what it would be, all right: a big resounding "yes."

And he also knew that tonight she'd be in his bed again, not Chandler's.

There was no controlling Lil. He had no more sway over her than he did the weather.

She was, in fact, a force of nature.

He pulled out his fixings bag, started to roll a quirley, and then remembered himself. "Do you mind, ma'am?" he asked the woman at the end of the table.

"I certainly do, although what good it will do, I don't know," she said huffily.

She aimed her stare at the other side of the table, where a cowhand had already lit up and was talking to a tablemate, his back to her. "It was kind of you to ask, however. You're more of a gentleman than *some* people in here."

"I'll just leave you folks to it, then," he said as he rose, his tobacco pouch in one hand and his hat in the other.

He flipped a generous twenty-five-cent tip to the serving girl on his way out the door, strolled up the street to the hardware store's front, and pulled up a nail keg.

He sat, his eyes on the saloon and its connecting

hotel/dining room, and built himself a smoke. It was dark by this time, and the lights shone brightly in the downstairs windows and flickered on and off, here and there, upstairs in both buildings.

He wondered if Lil had told Chandler that she'd marry him yet.

He considered just riding out of town.

And then he pictured Lil in his mind, every smooth and poreless inch of skin, every swell and dip of her form, and knew he had to have her, even if it was only one more time.

He could always leave in the morning.

After all, he didn't want to stick around for the wedding and the mess that would inevitably follow. There was always a mess, wasn't there?

It was Lil's way: the way of the thunderstorm, of the twister, of the earthquake.

Once she set herself in motion, there was no way of holding her back until she got what she wanted.

Yes sir, a real force of nature.

11

"Yes, David," Lil murmured over the low flower centerpiece between them. She lowered her eyes almost shyly and added, "I should be proud and pleased to be your wife."

David Chandler took her hand gratefully and bent forward. It was a good thing they hadn't been served yet, or his tie would have gone directly into his soup.

"Lily, my love," he said, bringing her hand to his lips. He kissed it gently. She smelled of jasmine. The scent of her was intoxicating, titillating, irresistible, as if just the sight of her wasn't enough. "Thank you, my darling," he whispered. "You've made me so happy . . . I don't have the words."

Without a word, she leaned forward, too, and placed her other hand on top of his. She gazed deeply into his eyes, then whispered, "And David, you don't how happy you've made me, just by asking."

The waiter arrived with a platter. Of all the damned timing! But he didn't even flick his eyes away from hers. "We will be good together, my love," he said. "You'll see."

"Well, dearest darling," she said, smiling as they broke apart and leaned back for the waiter, "I know my life will be incredibly enriched just by having known you."

Slocum ground out his fifth quirley of the evening just as David and Lil came out onto the street and started over toward the saloon.

He sat and watched as they stopped for a moment on the sidewalk, kissed, then parted. Chandler went in through the front doors of the saloon; Lil went around the side, to the stage entrance.

Slocum guessed that Chandler had his answer, and that it had been yes. *Blast that Lily, anyway!* he thought with an angry shake of his head.

And then he wondered why he had any right to be mad at her. He wasn't the one who'd asked for her hand, was he? Hell, he ought to be feeling sorry for Chandler. He ought to be turning her in.

He ought to just go get on Panther and ride out of town and let them sort out this mess—or what was primed to become one—on their own. With that real nice Sheriff Kiefer to help them out.

But the moon wasn't full, not by a long shot, and he wasn't going to take a chance on laming his horse out there in the dark.

And then he was angry about that.

He snorted, shook his head, slapped his hands down on his knees, and stood up. Things being what they were, he supposed there was nothing to do but go watch the show.

"Slocum," he muttered to himself as he went across the way to join the crowd that was beginning to push through the batwing doors, "you are sure a prime-grade fool."

Bill Messenger waited until the show had started before he went inside. It was just as well. He squeezed himself into a dark back corner of the building.

Oh, he could see Lil all right, but there was no way she could see him over the glare from the footlights. There wasn't another lamp lit in the whole place, except for one back behind the bar, and that had been turned down low.

She was warbling a sad song, one he had forgotten the name of. Lord, nobody could sing a song like Tiger Lil. That voice was so sweet, so ingenuous and almost naive, that no one suspected the training that had gone into it. She'd told him, back when they were an item. She'd said that if you could hear the training, the voice wasn't trained well enough.

He didn't know that this was true, but whatever Lil did when she sang, it worked. He could almost fall in love with her all over again, even knowing what he did about her.

Almost.

That was the operative word. Right now, if she'd been close enough, he would have reached out and strangled her.

Maybe he would have kissed her first.

Maybe he would have kissed her after, when she was still and quiet, no longer able to confuse him with her lies, her sweet, sweet lies . . .

Lil finished the tune and burst into a more lively one. The audience sang the chorus along with her. He didn't, though. His eyes flicked over the crowd until he found the one—the one who as especially besotted with her this time. Not that they all weren't.

But this one was sitting right at the footlights at a private table. He was rich. His name was David Chandler. Oh, he'd been keeping an ear to the ground ever since he came into town. This was just the first time Messenger had seen Lily's new target.

He supposed that he should feel pity for the man, considering what Lil likely had planned for him. But he felt nothing. All his emotions were tied up in Lil at the moment.

Maybe he'd kiss her before he killed her.

Charlie Townsend lay in his bed, slowly grinding his teeth.

What the hell had happened? Where the deuce was the sheriff?

Could he have missed Chandler? Really flat-out, plain missed him?

Those jaws kept working, grinding relentlessly. Jaw muscles clenched, released, clenched again.

He'd have to go back in the morning. That was all there was to it. He'd have to go back, get in closer this time, and take a chance on somebody recognizing him.

Damn it!

Slocum sat at the end of the bar, quietly nursing a beer and waiting for Lil's second performance. The rest of the crowd was drinking and whooping it up, and he'd lay good money that there were more than a few wishful innuendos about Lil being whispered behind cupped hands into eager ears.

He would have followed her back to her dressing room, but Chandler was staying put at his table up front, watching the stage entrance. Probably humming to himself, too, the poor bastard.

Chandler wasn't going to get lucky tonight, though. Not if Slocum knew Lil.

No, she'd be tapping as his door later tonight, not Chandler's. She'd make the bridegroom wait. And wait and wait and wait, while she was long gone, spending his money.

How many men had she taken like this, anyhow? It must be quite a number.

He gave a shudder, then signaled for a fresh beer.

It arrived a half second before Lil walked out on-stage again, in a new, bright blue, low-cut, spangled dress. As if one man, the crowd gasped, then fell into a nearly reverent silence.

Slocum reached for his new beer, barely noticing when the foam spilled down over his fingers. Despite everything he knew about Lil, despite all their history, she still took his breath away, too.

She started to sing.

Slocum allowed himself to be carried away by the sight of her and the sound of her for this one last performance. Tomorrow he'd leave, but tonight, there was only the music she made.

And later, there'd be only Lil, naked in his arms.

David Chandler let her voice wash over him like warm honey. They'd talked at dinner. She had agreed to marry him between her first and second shows, tomorrow evening. That last show would be her farewell performance.

He'd make an announcement, for the two or three fellows who hadn't heard it from the grapevine already. And then they'd stay the night at the hotel and drive to the ranch in the morning.

He wouldn't bother her tonight, although it was killing him. That was her one request: that they save themselves for their wedding night. And he would respect her wishes.

She couldn't know how grudgingly, though.

The only thing tempering his lust for her was the knowledge that after tomorrow night, she'd be his and his alone. No more low-cut gowns for the hordes of men who came to hear her sing. No more of those lascivious posters, such as the one that hung out front of this very saloon. No more peeks at her knees by cowboys, no more strangers' stares at the turn of her ankles.

He would be her sole caretaker, her only fanatic, and he alone would be the one to see her as they all imagined seeing her: nude, flawless, and beckoning him to her, only him.

Forever.

He silently vowed—for the hundredth time—that he'd remain an upstanding citizen. That he'd stay the man that he'd been—or at least, had been pretending to be—when Lil fell in love with him. That he would never revert back to his old ways, no matter how loudly they called to him.

My God, he thought with a sigh as he sat there, just across the footlights from her. *What did I ever do to deserve this, to deserve the likes of her?*

It seemed to him that there was nothing to this divine justice thing. Either that, or God wasn't paying attention.

And it was just as well that He wasn't.

When the last show was over, Bill Messenger waited around the saloon. He figured to give Lil enough time to get to her room and snuggle down for the night. And then he planned to sneak in and strangle her.

He hoped to hell she had a room with two doors, like his: one out to the hall, and the other one opposite, out to the wraparound second-floor porch. The latter would be a helluva lot easier to get into without being seen. You always took a chance when you tried from inside the building.

Or at least, so he supposed. He had been an inebriated almost-highwayman, not a hotel sneak thief.

He already had the murder weapon. Tucked into his back pocket was a green scarf. Her scarf. It was all she had left behind. Of her things, his things, what he had, for one fleeting, golden moment, considered to be *their* things.

As it turned out, they were all hers.

What a fool he'd been! And still, as he'd listened to her earlier, as he'd perched on the edge of his chair, rapt, he thought that maybe he could be forgiven, just a little.

Just a little.

David dropped Lil at her door after she'd finished the second show. It was hard, keeping him from coming in and staying. He was persistent, if nothing else.

But in the end, he acquiesced. He kissed her hand, she blushed—right on cue—and they both whispered, "Till tomorrow, my love," as they parted.

Lil watched until he had gone down the hall and turned the corner, then listened to the faint sound of his key in the door as he let himself into his rooms. Sighing in relief, she silently closed her door, then leaned back against it for a moment.

This time, she might have to stick around for a bit. David Chandler's holdings were far-flung and complicated. He was far from a simple man with a simple bank account that she could suck dry on her way out of town.

But it would surely be worth the effort of staying around town, as Mrs. David Chandler, for a week or two. At least, she hoped she could figure out the best way to sink her claws into his property in that amount of time. Half of her wished that this complication had been apparent right from the start. Maybe she wouldn't have tackled him in the first place.

But the other half of her liked the challenge of him—and separating him from his property. It was rather thrilling in a way, wasn't it?

She walked to her chifforobe, unhooking her dress as she went. And she was smiling. One more night with Slocum, then on with the show.

And the show always had to go on, didn't it?

Bill Messenger had bided his time, smoked a few cigarettes—the ground-out stubs of which now lay scattered about his boots, like last year's confetti—and waited until the lights were blown out in Lil's room. He sat on the second-floor wraparound balcony above the saloon, just feet from the little bridge that connected with the hotel's balcony.

He knew it was her room. Sitting in the shadows, he'd seen her, through the window, before she pulled the curtains, allowing the light to peer through only around the fabric's edges.

Now that the light was gone, he waited a little while longer. He'd thought about strangling her with

one of her own scarves but finally decided on a cord:
a cord in which he'd been methodically tying knots.
In prison, he'd heard that they were supposed to give
the cord a better grip or something.

Well, who was he to argue? It was his first time
killing anybody.

No, it was his first time to mete out justice. True
justice. An eye for an eye, right? Lil Kirkland might
as well have taken an ax to him the day she married
him. His life was over that day. Everything he'd
known, everything he'd worked for, all gone in the
blink of an eye.

If that wasn't murder, what was?

All right. Enough. She had to be asleep by now.
He stood up.

As he walked quietly over to the bridge, and to the
door that would let him into her room, he wondered
whether it would be better or worse if she woke while
he was doing it. Better, he thought.

He stopped outside her door and hugged the wall.

No, worse. He might be tempted not to do it. He
knew all too well the effect those eyes, that voice,
could have on him.

He dug into a pocket and pulled out two wires.
Who said that prison couldn't be an education?

Kneeling, he slipped the first wire into the lock,
felt it give to the pressure, then inserted the second
one. In three seconds flat, the door was unlocked and
creaking open.

He grabbed it, to silence it, and opened it more

slowly, applying upward pressure. It worked. The door opened as if it were on silent casters.

He slipped inside and let his eyes become accustomed to the deeper darkness within. He made out the shape of a bed, dimly made out rumpled covers. Reaching into his pocket again, he found the knotted cord.

12

David Chandler woke with the dawn, and the first thing he thought was *Today. Today my life will change forever.*

And it would change in the best way possible. Lil would be his. Those old urges—to return to his old, lawless ways—would vanish. He could at last enjoy the fruits of going straight, which he had at first attempted only in an effort to hide from the law. He'd thought it was temporary.

But he guessed that maybe, if you pretended to be different long enough, you actually changed. Could that be possible?

He rolled to his side and focused on the wall clock: 5:17.

Far too early. Too many hours of wakefulness before his betrothed—his betrothed!—was even awake, too many hours before she would be his. Too many hours for any one man to stand the waiting out of them.

At least, consciously.

He rolled onto his belly, hugged the pillow closer, smiled, and drifted off again.

* * *

Slocum, too, was awake.

He shifted his weight to reach for his smoking pouch, and in the process, woke Lil.

She shifted with him, allowing him to reach his fixings, and smiled sleepily. "It's morning," she whispered. "I should go."

But she didn't move.

Before he licked his quirley, Slocum paused to brush a kiss over her forehead. She was beautiful in the mornings, with no makeup and her hair mussed and the sheets rumpled around her. Absolutely beautiful. And today she was marrying another man.

How many times over was she guilty of bigamy? He didn't know. Even she had likely lost track.

Frankly, he didn't care. At least, not about the legalities part. He just worried for her, worried that she was so casual about it, worried that someday, she wouldn't make it out of town fast enough or that somebody would come out of her past to haunt her.

Nobody had, yet, and he supposed that made her even more fearless when she was pulling one of these scams. But still . . .

He gave a lick to his quirley and stuck it between his lips. Lil struck a match and held it to the tip. He inhaled, then exhaled a plume of smoke. Lil shook out the match, placed it in the little glass ashtray on the bed stand, then moved the ashtray to his belly. She sat up, letting the sheet fall away from her naked body.

Suddenly, he didn't want his smoke.

But he didn't stub it out, because a half second later, she was out of the bed and pulling on her night-gown and negligee. "Got to have a bath," she said, eyes on the gauzy belt she was tying. "My wedding day, you know."

I know, Slocum thought glumly—and a little an-grily, too. *And you have to scrub the scent of me off of you for another man.*

He didn't say a word, though. He just took another drag off his cigarette.

Lil looked up and cocked a brow. "You mad about something? I would have thought, after last night . . ."

"No," Slocum said, sitting up. He remembered the ashtray just in time. "Nothin'. And you were great last night, honey. The best."

She smiled. "I know. Somehow, you just bring out the class act in me."

Slocum had no reply for that.

Her brow creased prettily. "You okay, Slocum?"

"I've got to tell you something, honey," he replied. He didn't want to, but he'd put it off long enough. "David Chandler . . . isn't his real name."

She stared at him a moment longer, as if she were struggling to withhold a comment, and at last suc-cumbed. She said, "And Lil Kirkland isn't mine. What's the difference? Well, I'm off. It's been grand, darlin'. You've been grand."

She blew him a kiss, then turned and peeked out into the hall before letting herself out of the room.

Slocum muttered, "You bitch," before he stubbed out his smoke and flopped back onto the pillows.

It didn't help. They still smelled hauntingly of Lil's perfume. And he still hadn't told her the truth about her fiancé.

"Aw, hell," he grumbled, and tried to go back to sleep.

Charlie Townsend woke before the dawn and was already dressed, fed, and outside, saddling his horse.

Tom Lauden, one of the newer men, wandered into the barn and began throwing brushes into an empty bucket. He asked, "What you wantin' me and Fred to do today? We figured that if you was to come with us, we could mayhap get part of the old run-in shed fixed. Dang thing's cavin' in on the horses that are brave enough to get near it."

Charlie kept his eyes on the cinch he was tightening. "Got something else to do. You and Fred go on ahead."

Tom shrugged and walked back outside, the bucket swinging noisily in his hand. "You're the boss."

Not really, Charlie thought. *Not yet.*

But he had, at least, convinced himself sometime during the night that he could get the Circle C back all on his own. Sure, it was true he had no money, but that old prick at the bank, Baskin, could probably be talked into giving him a loan, especially once Chandler was dead. It wasn't like he was a stranger, was it?

And besides, who else would want the place?

Baskin would have to be loco to think he could find another buyer.

Charlie figured he could just go back to business as usual. He'd fire about half the men, cut back the salaries of those who stayed, sell off most of the cattle and hogs . . .

He could go back to his old ways, and he could scrape by.

He truly thought that he could kill Chandler with no one the wiser. It hadn't been all that hard to convince himself that everything would work out just fine.

Just fine.

He led his horse out into the yard and mounted up. He touched the butt of his rifle, just to make sure it was there, just to make sure it was real and that he wasn't dreaming all this.

And then he rode out, a thin smile, bordering on crazed, spreading his narrow lips.

"I've changed my mind, darling," David Chandler said to Lil. It was ten thirty in the morning, and she had just answered her door, wrapped in a damp bathrobe and holding one turbaned towel to her head and a second to her throat.

She cocked her head. "About what, David?"

He took her by her shoulders and planted a kiss on her sweet lips. "I can't wait until this evening. I want to get married now. Right away. I've already got the preacher."

Lily gasped in true surprise. "What? Before breakfast? Now? But I'm not dressed! I'm not ready! I'm not—"

"Nonsense!" He looked at his watch, grinning like a fool the whole time. He'd been grinning ever since he thought this up. He couldn't help himself. "I'll give you ten minutes to get ready, my love, and to bring your pretty self downstairs."

"But—" she began, but he cut her off with another kiss.

"Ten minutes, darling, or I'll bring the whole troupe up here!"

He left her standing in shock and went whistling down the corridor.

Bill Messenger was on the downstairs porch, whittling mindlessly at a piece of pine and trying to figure out what was going on inside. He'd lost his chance last night, and he'd be damned if he'd miss it again today.

Course, he had to wait for the stupid bitch to wake up. She hardly ever got up before noon, if he remembered rightly.

He'd thought about going to the upper porch, going to her room again, but it was broad daylight. Too many eyes watching, too many ears listening.

And then again, she might not be there.

Why the hell would she go off to Chandler's room before they were married? Lord knows she had never come to him till it was all done, tied up neat and legal. This irritated him for some reason. It made him oddly jealous, and he didn't like the feeling.

But then he heard David Chandler's voice from inside the hotel. He turned his head and saw Chandler talking to some big cowhand, inside the lobby.

Maybe Lil would be home after all.

Casually, he dropped his chunk of pine—which had failed to form into anything, but only gotten smaller—and kicked it back under his chair. He folded his knife and settled it home in his pocket, leisurely stretched his arms, and stood up.

He'd go right through the lobby, that was it. He'd go through the lobby and up the stairs, knock at her door, and when she answered, he'd shoot her in the face.

No, check that. He'd go to his room first and get himself a pillow, and wrap it around his hand and his gun. He'd heard that was good for muffling the sound of gunshots. Got feathers all over the place, but he supposed that was the price you paid.

He grinned.

See? Prison had turned out to be a fine training ground.

For some things, anyhow.

Lil didn't notice the sound of Bill Messenger's boots going past her room, to his. She was too busy, hurrying into her dress.

Of all the crazy ideas! She never thought she would have to get married with wet hair, of all things! She would have been more angry at David, save for the thought of how very rich he was going to make her.

Earlier, she had looked up from her dress, which she was hooking at the time, when she heard Slocum's boot steps headed the other way, past her room. She would have known his step anywhere.

For a just a fraction of a moment, she considered bursting out into the hall to stop him. But, to tell him what? He didn't approve of this wedding, anyhow.

For a moment, she paused with her hand on the latch, then decided to let it pass. Feverishly, she finished hooking her dress.

Just three minutes to go.

How she hated to rush like this! She'd already scraped her damp hair into some semblance of fashion, helped tremendously by a very large, plumed hat. Quickly, she dotted her lips and cheeks with rouge, then pulled down the hat's short veil.

One minute. If she knew David, she'd best get downstairs, or he'd be rapping at her door any second. That wouldn't do, on this of all days!

Briefly, she wondered if Slocum would be present for the ceremony. Secretly, she hoped he would, even if he only listened from the other room.

It made her feel just grand, being wanted by so many—and actually *had* by so few.

She took a quick inventory. Something old—her mother's hankie—something new—the engagement ring David had slipped on her finger the night before—something borrowed—well, she'd figure that out later—and something blue. She fingered the turquoise bracelet she wore.

All set.

She squared her shoulders, straightened the bodice of her light pink gown—no white for this bride—took a deep breath, and let herself out into the hall.

Everything was falling into place. Just a little sooner than expected, that was all, but she could cope with it.

She smiled. She always had coped and made do, hadn't she?

In fact, she'd "made do" so well that, at last count, her savings accounts at the First National Bank of Boston, the Citizen's Bank of Rhode Island, and four others carried a combined balance in excess of $654,000.

She didn't need to do this for the money anymore. She hadn't had the need for some time. She just enjoyed the sport.

Humming softly, she started toward the landing.

13

Charlie Townsend, obsessed with his goal, rode into town the back way and tethered his horse in the alley behind the hotel.

He wasn't quite certain just how he was going to pull this off, but he knew he would. It seemed as certain to him as the rising and setting of the sun. It was the natural order of things, for him to kill either Chandler or, at least, this . . . woman.

He supposed the first thing to figure out was their whereabouts.

He knew where Chandler stayed when he came to town, anyway—the hotel, in room twenty-five, which was actually a suite. He'd try there first.

He entered the service door to the hotel and slipped to the landing of the back stairs without anyone the wiser. It seemed that God was smiling on him, as if this was meant to be. He continued up the steps to the landing and crept to Chandler's door.

He touched his gun a little nervously, then with more confidence. Wasn't he doing God's work? He blinked rapidly. Yes, that was it. God's work! The Lord was making him a path, a clear path to his goal!

This thought gave him a great deal of comfort that

he hadn't thought he needed. The Lord had never been on his side before, had He? But it felt awfully good to have Him watching over him now.

Chandler was already dead and didn't even know it. Charlie was going to smite him, that was it. Just like in the Bible. Because Chandler had tripped to a female lie, to the temptations of Lilith and the fruit of Eve, he had to die.

Charlie, not quite sure what to do to acknowledge this unexpected divine intervention, finally crossed himself, like the Mexican hands did. Then, his right hand on his gun's butt, he put his left on the door's latch.

Around the bend in the hall, Bill Messenger stood in Lil's empty room, glowering.

Damn it!

Messy bed, tepid water in the tub, hairpins scattered . . . She'd left in a hurry, but she hadn't bothered to take her belongings with her. Could she know he was in Poleaxe and looking for her? He didn't see how. He'd sat far in the back of the saloon last night, in a dark corner. She couldn't have spotted him.

And besides, she gave no sign.

So what had spooked her out of her room in such a rush?

He started toward the landing. This time he'd use the front stairs. At this point, he didn't much care who saw him.

*   *   *

By the time Bill Messenger had rounded the landing and started down the stairs, a puzzled but determined Charlie Townsend was exiting David Chandler's empty rooms. He stood in the hall for a moment, trying to decide between a rock and a hard place, and finally chose the hard place.

He turned and crept back down the service stairs, let himself out the back door and into the alley.

Then, moving slowly, trying to act casual although there was no one there to see him, he sauntered around the building.

When he stopped with a start at a dining room window, he knew he'd chosen the right way. He pulled back immediately and flattened himself against the building. Tiny, barely noticed beads of sweat were already forming on his forehead.

Chandler was in there, surrounded by other men standing in a group in the center of the room, big as life.

As certain as death.

Charlie Townsend's fingertips tapped nervously on the butt of his gun. He could do it now. His horse was only twenty feet or so away, around the back of the building. And it seemed to him oddly preordained. God was on his side, after all, he reminded himself . . .

Quietly, resolutely, he drew his gun.

Bill Messenger stood in the lobby, his hands balling into fists as he watched Lil—her back, anyway—join

some well-dressed yahoo in the dining room. A
preacher was in the crowd. She was up to her old
tricks, for sure.

A tall, rugged man leaned in the doorway to the
dining room. He was rolling himself a quirley, and he
didn't look very happy about something. Messenger
wondered if he hated weddings or if he'd got himself
a bad batch of tobacco.

It didn't take long for the question to be answered.
The man looked into the dining room at Lil's back
and scowled. It was weddings then, and most probably Lily's in particular. Maybe he'd been past grist
for her marriage mill.

No, not that. If she'd married the tall man, he'd
have killed her by now. Or gone for the law. Something.

But all he was doing was watching the wedding
party arrange themselves for the ceremony. He didn't
look too happy about it, but that was all he was doing.

The happy couple was in place in the room's center, it having been cleared of tables for the occasion.
The few guests, nearly all men, had taken their seats,
and the preacher began to speak in low tones.

He had a clear line of fire to the side of Lil's head.
Slowly, he eased his gun free of its holster.

"Do you take this woman, in sickness and health,
in . . ."

The preacher's words turned into a meaningless
background drone when Slocum saw the man at the

window. And not just the man. The gun he was slowly bringing up. The gun that was aiming for Chandler's—or Lil's—head.

He drew without a thought, so fast that it startled even him, and was rewarded with the sound of a window shattering. No man, no gun.

But something about that shot had sounded odd. Part of the sound had come from behind him. Was that possible? He wheeled, but there was no one there, only the door swinging shut. And then hands seized him, and only then did he realize that Chandler was down, his head haloed by a pool of blood.

"Hey!" Slocum shouted as he shook off—or tried to—the hands that gripped him. He knocked one man across the room and shoved another into a table, but there were too many of them. Hands tore his gun away, held his arms, and then somebody slugged him.

"You idiots!" he shouted, working his jaw from side to side. That had hurt! "There was somebody at the—"

Somebody slugged him again, and this time it took its toll. He slid into unconsciousness.

"David! David darling!" Lil cried, and she meant it. She didn't know if the ceremony had gone on long enough for it to count. And David surely wouldn't go through it again. He was as dead as a stump.

Damn it, anyway!

"Help me!" she wailed. "Help him, somebody!"

A portly man put his hands on her shoulders and

gently drew her away. "There, there, missus," he whispered. "I'm afraid nothin' can be done for Mr. Chandler."

Careful to keep putting up her show, Lil turned and clung to him, sobbing. Had he said *missus*? She turned on a fresh well of waterworks. "David, oh, my David!"

Over his shoulder, she saw the broken window. When had that happened? She never paused in her wailing, though.

"Who would do this?" she cried. "Who would shoot my darling?"

"They got him, ma'am," said another voice, close behind her.

"It was that Slocum character," said the desk clerk, who had been excused from his duty to attend the wedding. "They hauled him out. Guess you didn't notice."

"S-slocum?" she sniffed. There was something rotten in Denmark, but she'd be damned if she knew what it was.

"Yes, ma'am," said the first voice. He sounded proud of himself. "Caught him with his gun in his hand. Sheriff Kiefer will call it . . . whatyacall. An open-and-closed case."

"He had a gun in his hand?" she sniffled, not quite believing what she heard.

"Can't you smell the gunsmoke?" the man asked, then tempered it with, "Sorry, ma'am. Didn't mean to be cross with you. I'm right sorry about your husband."

Lil still didn't look at him. She buried her face deeper in the fat man's lapel and wailed, "But the preacher didn't finish the ceremony!"

The Reverend Stuart's voice floated to her with the message she'd been hoping for. "It doesn't matter, Mrs. Chandler," he said gently. "You and Mr. Chandler signed the papers before the ceremony, remember?"

"We—we did?" she managed to get out.

"There, there," the reverend continued. "You're bound to be upset and mixed up at a time like this. May I help you to your room?"

She nodded into the fat man's lapel. "Yes. Yes, please. I want to be alone in my grief."

The preacher took her under his arm and guided her toward the stairs, offering his handkerchief along the way. "I can assure you, Mrs. Chandler, the wheels of justice turn swiftly here in Poleaxe. This Slocum will be punished for what he has done." They started up the stairs.

"Are you certain it was this Slocum?" she asked weakly through the tears. "I should hate to see an innocent man punished for something he didn't—"

"We all saw him, Mrs. Chandler."

Lil began to sob anew, although for a different reason than the reverend thought.

* * *

Bill Messenger didn't stop running until he reached the livery stable.

And when he looked back over his shoulder, he saw, of all things, the tall man being dragged out of the hotel and toward the jail!

Bill leaned back against the livery wall and sighed. There was no one coming after him? Nobody?

He even allowed himself a half smile.

But it went as quickly as it had come when he remembered that the bridegroom had fallen, not the bride. Was his aim truly that bad?

Charlie Townsend couldn't believe his luck.

He'd ridden out past the town and over the rise, and as far as he was aware, not a soul had spotted him. Of course, he had a new crease in his shoulder, courtesy of one of those two inside the building. One of those two with guns, aimed right at him, it seemed.

He also had a face full of glass, but that was easy enough to remedy. After he got another two or three miles from town, he'd stop and get it all picked out. He'd use the mirror from his shaving kit.

Of course, the whole thing had been bad timing. He had no way of knowing whether his shot had hit home. At least nobody suspected him of being up to no good, because nobody was chasing him.

But it was driving him crazy, not knowing if he'd taken down Chandler. Almost as crazy as the pain in his shoulder and his face.

Well, screw another two or three miles. He'd best take care of himself right here and now.

He reined in his horse, dismounted, and pulled his shaving kit from his saddlebags. Good thing he insisted that all the hands carry food, water, basic medicines, and toiletries with them at all times. You never knew when you might be trapped out in the nowheres by a sudden sandstorm or a hellacious downpour.

He picked the glass from his face and scalp and mopped up the blood before he took a look at his shoulder. As he suspected, it has just creased the meat.

He slathered it with unguent, bound it up with his neckerchief, rolled his sleeve back down, then stitched his shirt with a needle and thread. Nobody'd be the wiser.

Well, except for his face.

But most of the cuts were up high, on his forehead. He put his hat back on and painfully pulled it down low, inspecting himself in his shaving mirror. He could pass, he figured. Especially if he waited until after nightfall to ride in. He could go directly to his quarters, and nobody would bother him.

Nobody'd be the wiser.

He just wished he knew whether his slug had hit home, that was all.

Well, he supposed he'd find out. Tonight or tomorrow, he'd know something.

14

Slocum woke up in the Poleaxe jail, slung uncomfortably over a cot. A stained pillow and a couple of blankets had been tossed in after him and lay scattered and askew on the dirt floor of the cell.

With some difficulty and a great deal of pain, he craned his head back and looked at the desk. Sheriff Miles Kiefer—he supposed—was there with his feet propped up, and he looked self-satisfied and smug.

Slocum wanted to hit him. Course, that would have been something of a problem, what with the sheriff being at least ten feet away from his reach, even if he were standing up, even if somebody hadn't busted one of his ribs with a well-placed kick. But he still wanted to slug him in the worst way.

Memories were beginning to leak back into Slocum's mind with all the rapidity of molasses in January, but he did recall a few things. Slocum asked, "You're Kiefer, right?"

"Last time I checked." Kiefer lifted his head from the papers he'd been staring at. "Welcome back, Slocum," he said. "Proud of yourself?"

"Did I get him?" Slocum said, and was surprised when his voice came out in a croak.

"Deader'n dirt," the sheriff remarked with no emotion. "You could've picked a better spot to do it, though, if you were to ask me."

Slocum sniffed. "If I'd'a waited to go outside and shoot him, he would'a already shot Chandler." He looked away. "Course, he shot Chandler anyhow, but that was only because my aim was off. Must'a been the glass that done it. And why the hell you got me locked up when you should be out lookin' for him? Hell, I'll go with you!"

Slocum started to stand up, but Kiefer said, "Hold on." And Slocum did.

Slocum cocked a brow. "Why?"

"Because you shot David Chandler, Slocum. I got at least eight or ten witnesses to the fact."

"You're loco, Sheriff! Didn't nobody but me see that yahoo at the window? Or the feller standin' behind me on the stairs?"

Kiefer shook his head. "They only seen you, with that Colt in your hand, still smokin'."

"Well, of *course* it was smokin'!" Slocum shouted. "I just shot the man at the window! Hell, I blew the glass out of it, and I'm damn well sure I hit him, at least! Anybody check for a body in the alley, or at least a blood trail?"

But the sheriff wasn't having any of it. He gathered his papers, neatened them into a stack, and slid them into a desk drawer without a word passing his lips.

"Damn it, man!" Slocum insisted. "Answer me!"

The sheriff stood up, settled his hat on his head,

and walked to the door. "Night deputy'll be comin' in soon. Name'a Josh Childers. Me, I'm gonna make my rounds, then drop into the hotel for some dinner. Josh'll bring you yours."

Slocum watched the sheriff's back disappear and the door close behind him. Having already met the night deputy, Slocum couldn't exactly say he was looking forward to the pleasure of his company, but he supposed another body in the room—any body—would be an improvement. Wind whistled thinly through the boards that made up the building's walls, giving the place an eerie feel.

He wondered what Lil was up to—other than counting her money, that was. He wondered who it had been to actually file charges against him. Surely Lily would know that he couldn't have done this!

Well, maybe he could, he thought. But he'd expect her to defend him, damn it.

Almost an hour passed before he heard spur-bearing boots clinking and thumping on the walk outside, and the door creaked open. Deputy Josh Childers appeared in the doorway, a dish towel–shrouded tray balanced on one hand.

"Figured you'd be in here long before this," the deputy said by way of a hello. "You're nothin' but trouble. Told the sheriff so, myself. Fit for nothin' but the hangman's noose. And don't you worry, we got plenty of rope around town."

"Thank you, son," replied Slocum. "I've been comforted in my hour of need."

He watched Childers set the tray on the desk and pull out a small folding table, which he set up against the outside bars of Slocum's cell.

"You expect me to eat through these bars?" Slocum asked.

"If you want to eat anything at all, that's how you'll have to do it," said the deputy as he fetched the covered tray. "Mind you don't bust none'a the hotel's dishes, now. We'll take it outta your hide!"

Frowning, Slocum dragged his cot over to the bars and sat down opposite the table where rested his dinner, which turned out to be roast beef with potatoes and gravy, with side dishes of peas and applesauce and another with three biscuits and two small pots, one filled with honey, the other with butter.

At least they fed their prisoners well in Poleaxe, he thought. Including the ones they planned to hang.

With some difficulty, he began to eat.

Lil took her dinner in her room, Walter, the desk clerk, having offered to bring her something. "Everyone is being so nice," she had sniffed into her hankie when he'd come rapping at her door a half hour ago.

"There, there, Miss Lil," he'd muttered later, when he'd arrived, tray in hand. She'd been standing at her window at the time, her back toward him and her face hidden by the curtains, while he set out her dinner on the little table in her room. "There, there," Walt said. "The town'll see that you have everything you need. Anything at all."

"Anything except David," she'd snuffled into the hankie in her fist.

And then she felt him behind her, although he didn't put a hand on her. Was he trying to decide whether to touch her arm, to give her some modicum of physical comfort along with the emotional support he'd already offered?

Lord, she hoped not. As it turned out, he didn't lay so much as a finger on her.

She heard him step back, then say, "If there's anything else you need . . ." and slip from the room. Coward.

Of course there was something else she needed! But not from the likes of him.

Slocum would be more like it, but Slocum was cooling his heels up the street in the jail. Had he really, truly done it, the way they said? She could scarcely believe what she'd been told, but so many witnesses couldn't all be mistaken, could they?

Still, deep in her heart—if she, indeed, had one— she didn't believe it. Slocum wouldn't have killed David. And Slocum especially wouldn't have killed him in front of a roomful of witnesses!

Her meal half finished, she crumpled her napkin between both hands, then threw it down. She wasn't going to let them hang Slocum for some . . . some . . . some trick of the light, some sort of mass hysteria! But what could she do?

She began to pace her room, and she paced it through the day and into the night. At long last, she stopped. She'd get him free if she had to break him out of jail herself!

It likely wouldn't come to that, though, she thought as she grabbed her handbag and started down the stairs toward the lobby. After all, David had practically run this silly excuse for a town. But now David was dead, and she was in charge!

"Ma'am?" the night clerk said as he tried to bolt to his feet, and fell halfway over in the process. "Can I get you something, Missus Chandler?"

She didn't answer, and she didn't give him time to ask twice.

She was already out the door.

Charlie Townsend had arrived back at the ranch without incident, had put up his horse, and quickly retired to his little house.

Now he sat in the darkened front room, staring toward town through a window as he carefully cleaned his gun.

The scent of gun oil always cleared his head.

It didn't matter that he'd blown out the lights. He could have cleaned that pistol in the dark of night, deep down in the belly of a well if he had to.

And he'd had to do just that more than once, back in the war.

Those were the days, he thought. Although it didn't cross his mind to wonder why. Nor did it cross his mind to theorize on just why he was picking this moment to think about the war. Although it would have been obvious, had he chosen to mull it over.

War was legalized murder, a time when you were lauded for killing as many of your fellow men as you could, so long as they weren't wearing the same color uniform as you did. And he was preparing to laud himself for just the same thing.

As soon as word came.

He squinted at the clock across the room, failed to read it in the dim light, shrugged, and resumed putting his gun back together.

He'd really expected somebody to come tearing into the yard by this time of the evening. Actually, he'd expected somebody to come tearing in hot on his heels. But enough time had passed since he got home that he figured he was safe and blameless, and had pulled it off, after all.

Unless he'd missed.

Unless David Chandler was sitting upright in that saloon right now, listening to hell's own harlot sing.

He tossed aside his gun, only half reassembled, and walked to the window. Eyes straining, he tried to bore a hole through the distant rolls of land, to see far away, to town.

Were there riots in the streets?

Was a posse forming in front of the sheriff's office?

Or were they selling tickets to that whore's performance hand over fist?

Charlie's hand let go of the curtains he'd swept aside, and he let out a long sigh, then turned away. He walked back to the little washroom, turned up the lamp, and stared at himself in the badly silvered mirror hanging over his washbasin.

Of course, the light wasn't so good in here, but he was fairly certain that you couldn't tell how badly he'd cut his face this afternoon. The human body was a wondrous thing, fixing itself like that. And it had helped that he'd stopped and picked out the glass right off, like he had.

Between me and God, we'll take care of business, he thought with a smile. He felt a slight sting, but his wounds didn't open.

The smile stretched into a grin.

There was a sudden commotion outside. *They've come,* he thought.

He was right.

When he trotted out into the yard, he found Jess, owner of the livery, and two other men from town just climbing down off sweat-soaked horses, and two of the Circle C men with them, casting anxious glances his way.

Chandler's buggy was behind them, pulled by the fancy trotting mare of his, the one he'd called Acey. The seat was empty.

"Charlie . . . um . . ." said one of Chandler's men. Well, his men, now.

"What's happened?" Charlie asked. His eye

caught Jess's, and he frowned. Convincingly, he hoped. "What is it, Jess?"

"It's Mr. Chandler, Charlie," Jess said as he handed his mount's reins to one of the Circle C riders. "He's been shot dead."

Charlie damped down a sudden urge to hoot and forced his face into a sorrowful expression. "What?" he said. "*Our* Mr. Chandler?"

One of the men who'd ridden in with Jess came quickly to his side. "You'd best sit down now, Charlie."

He allowed himself to be walked to a barrel and slowly be seated on it. He'd rehearsed this in his mind so many times and so thoroughly that it wasn't as hard as he had expected it might be.

It was easy, actually.

But he felt a triumphant smile creeping too close to the surface of his face, and covered it with his hands.

"Tell me what happened," he said, through a picket fence of fingers, between the twin gags of his palms, through the hands that had so gallantly slain David Chandler. "Tell me the whole story. Tell me who done this awful thing."

15

Bill Messenger, sleeping quietly in the loft of the livery after sneaking in, was awakened by voices below.

At first, he couldn't make out what they were saying, and then it came to him, in a roiling burst of anger, that he recognized half the conversation—it was Lily's voice!

"I still say that you didn't have to hit him so damned hard, Slocum," she was saying. "He's only a boy, you know."

The man she was with—Slocum, apparently—replied with, "Shut up, Lil."

"Don't tell me to shut up!" Lil spat a little too loudly. "Who just broke you out of jail!?"

He heard straw being moved about by boots, heard the creak of a stall door, and the movement of hooves. He crept to the lip of the overhang and peered over.

"You did, darlin'," replied Slocum. And then Messenger suddenly recognized him; this was the man who had fired just as he had, the big man who was bent on killing Lil! Or Chandler. He wasn't sure. His blood froze in his veins.

"Then stop being so . . . so . . . so *Slocumish!*" Lil

fairly hollered. "Especially after I tippy-toed down the street with you! Especially since I got yanked into every alley and doorway along the route!"

Slocum wheeled toward her and pulled her into his arms.

And kissed her, hard.

Messenger's teeth clenched along with his fists. But he was madder at himself than at the couple below. Christ, he was thick as a plank if after all she'd done to him, after everything she'd put him through, he was still jealous!

Slocum released Lil, and still holding her close, he said, "You shouldn't have done it, Lily," so softly that Messenger, five feet overhead, barely heard him.

"Well, what was I supposed to do?" Lily snapped, her eyes flashing. "Let them hang you?"

"You could have spoken up for me," Slocum said and turned to start tacking up his horse. "That would have been plenty."

Lil crossed her arms over an ample bosom. "Didn't see you saying you wanted to stay put."

"You didn't give me much choice, did you?"

Lil shook her head. "All right. Come on. I'll say I captured you. Or recaptured you."

"Go back to the hotel."

She gave a little huff and said, "No. I'm staying with you."

Slocum turned around again. "Sure. You want to camp in the desert." Messenger heard him give out a quick snort. "I believe that, all right."

"Well, what am I supposed to do now?"

Slocum finished up and led his horse from its stall. It was a fine animal, if Messenger was any judge. And he was.

"You should have thought of that before," he said, his hand fisted with reins and resting low on the horse's withers. "Thanks, Lily. You're a peach."

He started to step up on his horse, but Lily stopped him. "Well, what are *you* going to do?" she asked, almost like a little girl.

"I'm going to try to figure out just what the hell is going on here," Slocum answered and dusted a kiss over her forehead.

"How can you do that from out of town?"

"I'll have to figure out a way, won't I?" he replied and swung into the saddle. "Do what I asked you. Don't forget."

Messenger jerked his head back, just in case, and managed not to rustle the hay he was lying on. He closed his eyes for a second and opened them to see Slocum mounted up and stopped at the barn's mouth. Lil was at the door, and she was peering out.

"All right," she said. "It's safe."

"Bye, baby," were the last words Slocum said before he rode out the wide doors.

Lil lingered for a moment, and while she stood there, Messenger wondered who the hell Slocum was. And what was he to Lil? He must be something special, for Lil to have broken him out of jail. The act was totally out of character for her.

Put him in jail, blackmail him, coerce him, cheat him: yes—but not do him a favor that might have put her in peril!

In fact, Messenger was so busy trying to riddle out this conundrum that he missed a perfectly good chance to put a slug into her lying, cheating, larcenous skull. She had slipped out the doors and away before he even thought of it.

He sighed heavily and rolled over, away from the overhang. Hands clasped over his chest, he cursed himself for an idiot and then cursed Lily for complicating things. If only she'd stood still for a second this afternoon, his bullet would have taken her out instead of Chandler. It was just like her, wasn't it?

The Slocum fellow had been shooting at the old man in the window. Messenger had seen him plainly—well, as plainly as possible through the warped window glass—from his vantage point behind Slocum at the bottom step of the stairs, and he had heard the old man's slug sing past his ears and bury itself in the woodwork.

Seemed like everybody in town had been gunning for the happy couple, one way or another.

That thought brightened him a bit, and he managed a grin.

Well, Slocum hadn't been aiming for Lily. Had the man at the window? Or had he been aiming for Chandler all along?

Messenger sighed. He supposed it didn't make

any difference. One way or another, Chandler was just as dead.

For a few moments, Messenger debated following Lil up to the hotel and trying again, but in the end, he did nothing but fall asleep.

Slocum rode out past the end of town, past the low rise where he'd seen the lone rider earlier, then rode on another couple of miles. He'd forgotten to remind the sheriff about that man and the shooting, hadn't he?

He shook his head. The sheriff hadn't exactly been eager for information, but then, Slocum himself had been pretty flummoxed by the situation, too.

But at least he'd asked Lily to check the alley, once it was light out. And he knew she would. If he'd hit the window—and he was certain that he had—the broken glass would be on the outside.

If the shooter had busted it, it would all be on the inside.

He hoped she'd find a blood trail, too.

He rode up to a small clump of palo verde, in the moonlight dimly yellow with spring blooms, and dismounted. After he led Panther under their shelter, he stripped the tack off of him, secured him for the night, strapped on his nosebag, then proceed to find himself enough fuel for a small fire. Not one big enough to be seen from very far off, but he had to have coffee. The deputy hadn't been much on offering it.

By the time he'd started a small blaze and set the
pot on, it was time to take the nosebag off his horse
and offer water, which he did. He rifled his saddlebags for the body brush and curry comb, but once he
found them he discovered that he didn't really need
them. Jess had taken better than average care of his
horse.

He patted the gelding on his glossy neck. "You're
in good shape, Panther," he said, a smile curving his
lips. "Right good shape!"

He gave the gelding a cursory currying over its
back and belly, just to scratch the places the saddle
had rubbed, then put his brushes away and sat down
by the fire.

Pouring out a cup of coffee, his mind turned again
to the morning's distant shooter. He'd been gunning
for Chandler, that was for certain. It boggled
Slocum's mind that with that evidence, nobody had
even looked at the window. Hell, if he'd been sheriff,
that would've been the first thing he would have
checked into!

Well, maybe the second or third.

But he would have looked, by God!

He shook his head and frowned. Hell, nobody—
besides the undertaker—had even checked the body,
insofar as he knew. That, at least, would have showed
somebody which side of Chandler the slug had come
from!

It hadn't come from his gun, he was sure of it.

He sipped his coffee and swore under his breath.

This was surely one hell of a pickle he found himself in.

One *hell* of a pickle.

Lil hadn't gone directly to her room.

She'd gone, instead, to the alley where Slocum
had told her to look for the broken glass. It was too
dark to see much of anything, but when she stepped
in front of the window, it gave a satisfying crunch
underfoot.

So Slocum had been right! There *had* been another shooter!

Why that knowledge should be so comforting to
her, she didn't know. After all, hadn't she busted
Slocum out of the hoosegow? That had been different,
though, she decided. She'd broken him out because
she knew, on the strength of his character, that he
hadn't done it. That he'd never do anything like that.

But now she had something tangible with which to
back up that feeling she had, to justify it. And she
wished she'd checked the alley before she'd barged
into the jail with her purse full of a loaded pistol and
her head full of righteous indignation.

She saw, then, that Slocum had been right to fuss
at her for doing it.

She'd been a fool! She had David's money,
David's . . . well, everything! And now she'd set
Slocum free. The sheriff wouldn't be happy about
that. And besides, how could she explain it? What excuse could she possibly have?

She stared in through the window that her husband's murderer had fired through to kill him, pictured David and herself, as they had been standing before the minister. And she smiled.

Good man, whoever you were, she thought.

And then she shook her head rapidly. *Stop congratulating yourself, girl,* she thought. *Slocum's in trouble, and now you've dug yourself in so far that it's up to you to get him clear of it!*

And, besides, she reasoned, David had laughingly told her that he figured he could get away with murder in this town if he wanted, just because he owned so much of it. What had he called it?

A "leading citizen's pass," that was it.

And she supposed that she had that pass, now.

Poor David.

Oh, well.

With a shrug, she turned back toward the street and was about five feet from emerging onto the boardwalk when she heard the hollow ring of approaching footsteps. Quickly, she turned and raced toward the back of the building, rounded the corner, and plastered her spine against the clapboards.

"I'll be damned," she heard someone mutter, and peeked around the corner. "I'll just be double damned."

It was the sheriff, she finally decided. She didn't know him well enough to recognize his voice, but she surely knew what that flash of a badge on his chest meant. And she heaved a small sigh of relief in spite of herself. She wouldn't have to tell him, after all.

And then she realized that telling him about the glass was the least of her worries. Why, he'd probably been up to her room already, looking for her! He'd arrest her the moment he set eyes on her.

No, no, she had the leading citizen's pass.

But she'd held a gun on the deputy!

Repeating, *leading citizen's pass, leading citizen's pass* over and over in her head like a mantra, she made her feet travel the rest of the way around the building to the staircase between the buildings and tiptoed silently up to her room.

Let the sheriff come. She'd think of something.

16

Once Jess and the other men from town had ridden out, a stoic but sniffling and obviously upset Charlie Townsend went back to his little cottage and sat down in his chair overlooking the window. He put an end to his pretense of holding back great emotion, and proceeded to wait.

He'd give Jess and his friends time to get back to town, and meanwhile, he'd decide what to do. His shot had come too late, for Jess had told him that now Lil owned the Circle C, damn her hide!

He had to figure out what to do about her. If he'd been smart, he would have aimed for her, not Chandler.

He'd sure loused it up, that was for certain.

He sat in the darkness, watching the men's horses pass over the hill and out of sight, and ground his teeth.

A female boss!

Not for long, if he had anything to do with it. No, not for long.

Miles Kiefer trudged slowly back to his office. This changed everything. He supposed he'd have to turn

Slocum loose again, damn his hide! Kiefer could handle a town where there was one killer on the loose—particularly if he was on his good behavior, as Chandler had been—but a whole town of them?

He opened the jailhouse door and stopped stock-still, staring.

Slocum was nowhere to be seen, and Josh was unconscious and locked in Slocum's cell!

Growling, "Sweet, sufferin' Jesus!" beneath his breath, he unlocked the cell and bent down to Josh. Shaking the boy—and finally dumping a couple of cups of cold water on his face—he finally roused him.

"What happened!" he demanded.

Josh looked up through bleary eyes. He seemed to be having trouble focusing, and Miles reached for the cup again.

But before he could once again dump the contents over Josh's face, Josh mumbled, "Don't. I don't know what happened, after Miss Lil came in. But don't douse me no more!" He rubbed at his face with one fist and propped himself up with the other.

Sheriff Kiefer put the cup down on a stool. "Miss Lil? Miss Lil was here?"

Josh nodded dully, then flicked droplets from his right ear.

"Dang it, boy, stay with me!" Miles insisted.

"Sure," his deputy muttered. "Whatever you say."

Miles shook his head, then took a deep breath and started over. "All right. Miss Lil was here. When?"

"Just before the ruckus started."

Miles didn't say anything, just kept staring at the boy.

"Oh!" Josh said, as if God had suddenly lit the heavens. "Miss Lil helped him get out!"

"That's what I was after, boy," Miles said. He stood up and took a couple steps back. "She say why she was doing it? Helping him, I mean," he added, when Josh's face started to go toward blank again.

Josh shook his head. "No, sir. Didn't say nothin'. Well, she said, 'Hello Josh,' when she come in. And 'Sorry, Josh,' when she pulled that little gun outta her purse."

"Surprised you, did she?" Miles asked.

"I'll say! Why, you'd never expect—"

"That's just the kind of thing that'll get you killed," Miles said, interrupting. "Women with guns, kids with knives, pet dogs carrying dynamite . . ."

"Huh?"

"Never mind."

Miles figured that Slocum was long gone by now. And why go and find him, when he'd already discovered that somebody else had been shooting at the same time as he? Or so it appeared, anyway. It had been too dark to see if there was a blood trail, but he'd figured to take a lantern back and look. No big toot to change plans just because of a little jailbreak.

Just the same, he believed he'd call on Miss Lil on the way back.

But Josh still sat in the cell, dripping slowly on the edge of the cot, like a retriever fresh from the river.

"Get a move on, boy," Miles said, his voice clipped. "Get out of there and get yourself dried off."

Josh stood up, eyes wide as saucers. "I ain't fired?"

"Not this time," said Miles. Grabbing a lantern off the wall, he let himself outside again, lit it, and started back down toward the hotel.

"What?" was the first thing out of Miss Lil's mouth when she answered his knock.

Miles Kiefer, sheriff of Poleaxe, pushed his hat back, folded his arms, and just stared at her. He'd left his lantern downstairs.

"Do you know what time it is?" she persisted. "You have your nerve, Sheriff, pounding on a new widow's door at six o'clock in the morning!"

"And might I say that you have your nerve as well, Mrs. Chandler, breaking a man out of jail barely an hour before dawn?"

Lil looked down her nose at him like he was some kind of bug. "Would it have been better if I'd done it at high noon?"

"No," admitted Miles, "but you do have to admit it made a pretty sentence."

He closed the door behind him and sat in the chair against the wall. He motioned her to sit, as well.

She reluctantly settled on the edge of the bed and asked in a kinder tone, "And just what do you intend to do about it?"

Miles rubbed his chin thoughtfully. It was plain she had the whole thing figured out. That was, about how she owned half the town now, and how he couldn't rightly arrest her. At least, not and keep his job past sunup.

So he tried something different. He reasoned with her.

"What did Slocum tell you?" he asked softly.

Lil seemed surprised by his question, but replied, "Just told me to look outside the window, downstairs. Told me to look for broken glass, of which I found plenty. You see, it proves—"

"The other man," Miles broke in. "I know. I remember him hollering something like it when he was in jail. Well, I've just been out there with a lantern. Found broken glass and blood, too."

Lil pulled herself up and stuck out that famous chest of hers. "Well, there! You see? He didn't kill my David after all!"

"Maybe so," said Miles, who stuck to his duty and did his best to ignore her bosom. "But that opens a whole new can of worms, Mrs. Chandler. For instance, if you didn't speak to Slocum after Mr. Chandler was hit, how'd you know to set him free? Why in creation would you break him out of jail when he was the single good suspect?"

She didn't reply, just looked at her knees, and this got Miles wondering.

He lowered his voice, leaned forward, and said, "Mrs. Chandler? Did you know Slocum before he came to town? I mean, did you know him from before?"

He watched the soft line of Lil's mouth go tense and then relax again. And at last she looked at him once more.

"Yes," she said, simply. "I knew him previously."

"And because of that—?"

"I knew he couldn't have killed my dear, sweet David," she said, and burst into tears.

Now, he hadn't really been expecting this—not at this stage of the game, at least—and it threw him completely off step.

He found himself handing her his handkerchief and saying things like, "There, there," both of which were totally foreign to him, but, considering the circumstances, seemed the only things to do and say.

Slocum, dozing beside his cold fire, was wakened by hoofbeats.

He roused enough to tell which way they came from and were headed, although he couldn't see the riders. He remembered that David Chandler lived out the way from which they were coming, and reckoned that those boys must have been sent to alert the ranch to Chandler's fate. At least, that was the first thing he thought of.

He sat all the way up and listened as the hoofbeats faded on their way to town, and then he rolled himself a quirley. There was some thinking to be done.

He hadn't shot Chandler. He was sure of it. But that stranger had come—and run off—in the direction of Chandler's ranch. Now, there were about eight million other places a man could get to by riding in that direction, but right at the moment, Chandler's ranch seemed the most likely.

Would one of his hands hate him enough to shoot at him twice in the same day?

No. Slocum didn't think so. After all, Chandler was reputed to be well-liked by everybody. Hell, Slocum had halfway liked him, himself, and he had several good reasons to hate the man! And he hadn't seen any of those grudging faces people made when they felt they were having to be nice to somebody, even after Chandler turned his back.

But still, there might be a grudge someone held. Chandler had to have bought his ranch from somebody, hadn't he? He had to have gotten his stock somewhere. And he did have a past. All kinds of things could hide in a man's past, things Slocum couldn't know.

He lit his quirley and took a deep pull on it, breathing out a dense cloud of smoke. It wasn't as if he could just ride into the ranch the next morning and start asking questions.

Lil had sure put him into a precarious position. He needed the sheriff now, or at least, he needed somebody! About all he could do in the present circumstances was hightail it and hope for the best.

But Slocum being Slocum, hightailing it was simply out of the question.

However, he still didn't come up with any options that were better. He finished his smoke, ground it out on the desert floor, lay back down, and tried to go to sleep. Maybe he'd come up with something when it got all the way light.

Slowly, Sheriff Miles Kiefer rode through the dawn, alert for the smallest spark of light, the tiniest out-of-place rustle, the merest hint of movement.

He'd headed this direction because, once Lil stopped crying, she'd admitted that Slocum had ridden off this way. Kiefer didn't believe Slocum's heading had anything to do with Chandler's ranch being out here. It was just that it had been the quickest way to clear the city limits.

He rode on, all his senses alert, although he sure wasn't coming up with any clues so far. And then, about halfway to the Chandler spread, he decided to investigate a clump of palo verde off to his left.

He rode at a slow walk closer to the trees, then stopped and started leading his horse, creeping closer and closer. Still nothing, no sign.

But then . . . did he hear the idle stamp of a horse's hoof?

He ground-tied his mount and moved forward again, and once he edged just past the perimeter of foliage, he heard something more concrete.

The click of a gun's hammer easing back.

He froze.

He whispered, "Take it easy, Slocum. I'm just here to talk."

There was a long silence, and then a voice from

the darkness said, "You might wanna drop that gun belt first, there, Sheriff."

Kiefer didn't argue. He did as he was told, although it did cross his mind, as his weapon and belt slid down to hit his boots, that Deputy Childers would surely get the shock of his young life when he found his body tomorrow. If he ever found it, that was. Josh wasn't all that smart, when you come right down to it.

Of course, considering that he'd walked right into an ambush, neither was he.

"Kick it clear," said the voice.

Kiefer did. And waited for the worst.

But the next words he heard were, "You wanted to talk? I'm listenin'."

Inwardly, Kiefer heaved a sigh, and then began. "I talked to Miss Lil. She admits she busted you out. I also took a look at that window. You were right, Slocum. Your shot hit the glass, and hit meat, too. There was blood. But I went down to the undertaker's place and had a closer look at Chambers's body. The shot that killed him came from your direction."

Kiefer half expected to be cut down where he stood, considering Slocum's reputation, but instead, Slocum suddenly came into view as he casually flicked a match and lit a quirley. Kiefer noticed the gun in his other hand, though. It was aimed at his heart.

"Sit down," he said, and Kiefer didn't argue.

Slocum held his match to a bit of kindling material at the edge of the fire, and soon they had a small blaze going. Kiefer noted that Slocum had made himself a small, homey camp for a man on the run.

"All right," Slocum said. "I fired once. How'd my slug land in Chandler's head and the window at the same time?"

Kiefer sniffed. "That's exactly what I was wondering."

17

"You know, Slocum," Kiefer said as they jogged back toward town, "I don't know if I should be the one to talk to Miss Lily. After what you told me, I'm of half a mind to wring her pretty neck."

Slocum hadn't told him all of it, not by a long shot, and he was glad he hadn't, if this was Kiefer's reaction to the little bit he'd let slip. Lil was a con artist and crooked as a corkscrew, but no women with a neck—and everything else—that pretty deserved killing. Period.

"I wouldn't go getting too charged up, Kiefer," Slocum said. "She's a creature of habit, that's all. The possibility does exist though. Thought you should know."

"That mayhap it was some poor cheated galoot out after her? Somebody out of her past?" Kiefer shook his head. "I highly doubt it. If there'd been a stranger in town, I'd'a known it. But there's something lunatic about this whole business."

Slocum blew air out threw his lips. "Kiefer, seems to me your town's been full of nothin' *but* strangers ever since Lil showed up."

"I meant suspicious ones," Kiefer snapped. "Don't take me for an idiot."

"I surely didn't," Slocum said. Kiefer was touchier than he'd thought. "Not for one minute. I was just pointin' out that one sheriff can't get a close look at every gaslight Johnny who wanders into his town to see the show. Especially if that feller don't want to be seen."

There was a pause, and then Kiefer said, "Oh. See what you mean. Sorry, Slocum."

"And your Mr. Chandler might have had more enemies than you know about," Slocum went on.

The sheriff grunted. "You know about that Dave Young business?"

"Huh?"

"Name he went by, back in Ohio. Wanted back there for murder and robbery."

"And you knew it?"

Kiefer shrugged. "You know how jurisdictions are out here, Slocum."

"Yeah. I knew him as Felix Hamilton," Slocum said. "Gambler. He killed my partner."

"Busy lad."

"Yeah."

They rode into town, and left their mounts at the livery, with the surprised Jess. "You sure you know what you're doin', Miles?" he whispered to the sheriff, just loud enough for Slocum to overhear.

"Pretty sure, Jess," Kiefer answered, and tossed his reins over. "Just put 'em up, all right?"

"All right," the stableman answered, but he slid Slocum a look that said, *I don't trust you any farther than I could toss this building*.

Slocum understood. He supposed.

Alongside Miles Kiefer, he left the livery and started up toward the hotel and saloon. In the early morning light he could only make out the toothy smile on the big poster of Tiger Lil and the whites of her eyes. He supposed he'd be able to make out the rest of her when he saw her in person, in just a few minutes.

And Christ, he had a hard-on just thinking about it! Damn her, anyway!

Over Jess's head, in the stable loft, Bill Messenger slept on in the hay. He moved a little when Jess dropped a bucket but otherwise was undisturbed.

He didn't know it, but this was likely the last good night's sleep he'd ever get.

Out on the Circle C spread, Charlie Townsend had fallen asleep in his rocking chair in front of the window. He slept more fitfully than Messenger, but he slumbered still. And he dreamt of what would come, when he owned the ranch again outright, when he could spend his days doing what he pleased and when every moment of the day wasn't dependent on David Chandler's whim.

Despite the unaccustomed and clumsy sleeping position, he slept pretty damned well, with a smile on his lips.

* * *

No one could have been more surprised than Tiger Lil Kirkland when she answered the rap on her door, only to find the sheriff and Slocum standing in the hall!

Her jaw dropped, and she found herself bereft of words. But the sheriff said, "You don't mind if we come in and talk for a spell, Miss Lil?" and moved on past her, right inside, without waiting for so much as a by-your-leave.

There was nothing she could do but step aside as the two men filed past her and pulled out chairs. Eventually, she closed the door and joined them, sitting primly on the edge of her mattress, her negligee pulled tight around her.

"Well?" she said, breaking the uncomfortable silence.

"Well, it's like this, Miss Lil," the sheriff started. "I mean, Mrs. Chandler."

Slocum sniffed at that, she noted.

"What I mean to say, Mrs. Chandler, is . . . we're thinking that maybe the shooter wasn't . . . wasn't exactly aiming for Mr. Chandler."

Lil cocked a brow. "And who, pray tell, was he aiming at?"

"Had the feeling he might have been aiming at . . . at you, ma'am," the sheriff said softly, while staring at the floor.

Lil rolled her eyes, but then Slocum spoke up. "Somebody from your checkered past, Lil. Somebody with a grudge."

She slid a quick glance to make certain the sheriff was still fascinated by the floor planks, then shot Slocum a look that should have withered any other man into abject silence.

But he didn't take the hint. He continued, "Did you see any familiar faces around Poleaxe, Lil? Besides mine, I mean."

Her eyes narrowed and she hissed, "Slocum!"

"He already told me some of your story, Mrs. Chandler," the sheriff said, finally looking up and right into her eyes. "We've got a murder to figure out, and it's not going to be any easier with some parties . . . hiding things. Things that might be important, I mean."

Lil didn't say anything, just nodded. She was too angry to say much of anything. The first chance she had, though, she was going to get Slocum alone, and she was going to give him an earful, all right!

"So did you notice anybody you knew in the crowd, Mrs. Chandler?" the sheriff continued. "Even just a glimpse, somebody you thought you saw. On the streets, in the saloon, in the hotel . . . anything?"

"No," she managed to bark out. "No one. May I go out to my ranch tomorrow?"

"Don't see why not," the sheriff said, then looked at Slocum.

"She's probably safer out there than in town," he drawled.

The sheriff nodded. "I agree. Mrs. Chandler, you go on out to the Circle C in the morning, then, and get settled in. But if you should remember anybody or anything at all, you tell me or Slocum. You understand?"

"I do, Sheriff," she said as she rose, giving them a not-so-subtle hint to leave.

Slocum was already on his feet, and the sheriff joined him. Slocum opened the door, but before the sheriff followed him out into the hall, he turned back and said, "Mrs. Chandler? I'm not so sure about you being safe anywhere at the moment. I'd like to ask Slocum to go on out there with you and stay on for a bit, until we get this thing settled. If you wouldn't mind, Slocum?"

Slocum nodded. "Fine by me."

Flatly, Lil said, "Certainly, Sheriff. Anything you say." That low bastard! If he thought he was going to come out to *her* ranch and live off the fat of the land, he was in for a surprise!

She added, "I'm sure I can find something to take up his spare time."

Slocum sent her a short but cocky grin, which she didn't return. She'd have him out all day fixing fences or breaking horses or whatever it was they did on ranches!

"Good enough," the sheriff said and quickly touched his hat brim. "I'll be in touch, ma'am." He walked through the door and down the hall, in step with Slocum. The two were deep in conversation as they turned to go down the stairs.

Men! she thought with a huff as she closed the door again. Someone trying to kill her? Madness! David Chandler surely had plenty of enemies to choose from!

Her lips tightened into a hard little line, she walked stiffly back to her bed, moistened her fingertips, and snuffed out her candle.

Crazy, that's what they were. Crazy!

"You sure I wouldn't be more help in town?" Slocum asked once they hit the sidewalk. He liked Kiefer, despite that badge on his chest, and frankly, he thought it was pretty far-fetched that Lil would come to any harm tucked away on the ranch. In fact, Kiefer was handing him a holiday on a platter! But still, he didn't take to the idea of just letting the killer roam free.

"No," Kiefer said. "But you can stay around till morning and leave with Miss Lil. Mrs. Chandler. I want you to go with me while I talk to those boys who were at the wedding. It's awful early. They'll still be tucked in for the night."

Slocum leaned against a porch post. "So, wake 'em up."

"I gotta be sheriff here later, too," said Kiefer.

"Right," replied Slocum, even though he was loath to admit it. "Don't suppose it'd do much good to go pokin' snakes when you don't have to."

Kiefer nodded, then pulled his hat brim down low over his forehead. "Care to have a beer with me before we start wakin' up people? They got a breakfast special. Not much, just all the free toast you can eat, but it's with jellies and such."

"Be pleased."

The two walked the short distance to the saloon, which was certainly a whole lot calmer than it had been when Lil was performing. Isolated little clumps and clots of men gathered at the bar and at a few of the tables. They spoke quietly, so the only sound in the place was a sort of wordless murmuring hum. Kiefer picked a table in the corner and signaled to the barman.

"Here's one we can talk to right now," Kiefer said as the bartender brought them a couple of beers.

Slocum recognized the man. He'd been at the wedding, too.

Slocum leaned back in his chair. "Go ahead, Kiefer," he said. "Amaze me."

The bartender looked up and frowned. "Hey! Ain't you the feller—?"

"Yes, Harry," Kiefer said with a wave of his hand. "But he didn't do it. I've come to ask you if you saw anybody standing behind him, or up on the stairs."

Harry made a face and scratched the back of his head. "There was a shot, and I turned around, and he—" He pointed a finger at Slocum. "—was the only man I saw."

"Thanks, Harry," said Slocum, and reached for his beer. "You been a lot of help."

"You see anybody before that, Harry?" asked the sheriff.

"Didn't look. Hell, I was too busy lookin' at Miss Lil. Reckon everybody was."

"You see anybody at the window across from Slocum?"

Harry knotted the bar towel in his fingers. "I told you, Kiefer. All I seen was Miss Lil."

Harry went back to the bar, and Slocum said, "That's the trouble with pretty women. They blind all men."

Kiefer had no reply.

18

Slocum made the rounds of the wedding guests with a stoic Kiefer and a rattled Deputy Childers. Seemed that Childers still thought Slocum was the culprit and made no bones about it.

He was way too happy to mention this fact to anyone who would listen, to the point where Kiefer finally said, "Josh, either you shut up right now, and no more about your theory, or you're going to be cleaning spittoons your whole life. You got a handle on what I'm saying?"

The boy had the courtesy to look a bit chagrined and spoke of it no more. But he still eyed Slocum in a most suspicious way, and behind the sheriff's back, glowered at Slocum outright.

Not that Slocum much cared. Oh, it irritated him some, but he wasn't about to coldcock a kid just for having the wrong idea. Even if he was being a horse's butt about it.

When they'd interviewed all the guests and each one, to a man, had said that he hadn't been looking at the doorway or the window, only Miss Lil, Slocum wasn't surprised. That's what they got for not having any female guests at the wedding. A woman would have had the sense to look around a little. And then he had an idea.

"Kiefer," he said as they left the last attendee's place of business, "wasn't there a single woman in the place? I can't remember for the life of me."

Kiefer stopped walking. "A woman? Why a woman?"

"Because a female wouldn't have been so . . . enchanted with Lily's charms. A woman would have paid more attention to her surroundings," Slocum explained. "Leastwise, I think so."

"The mayor's wife!" Josh practically shouted in a fit of epiphany. "I was pretty sure the mayor and his wife were gonna go!"

Kiefer cocked a brow, and even Slocum tipped his head and put an arm around Josh's shoulders, saying, "Maybe you're not such a rattlebrained idiot after all, boy."

Josh wiggled out from beneath his arm and shot him a look meant to wither, but Slocum just laughed.

"Let's go," Kiefer announced, and the three of them set off for the mayor's house.

Mayor Tinny lived in a modest adobe at the edge of town, and his wife—a broom in her hand and an apron tucked round her ample waist—answered the door.

She looked surprised to see who her callers were.

"Sorry to bother you so early in the morning, Mrs. Tinny," Kiefer began, "but we wanted to ask you a few questions about yesterday. At the wedding?"

She only had eyes for Slocum, and she appeared terrified, as if she thought he would murder her at any moment. "Why . . . why . . . why is he out of jail? On the streets!" she asked, and gripped that broom like a weapon.

"Calm down, ma'am," Kiefer soothed. "The evidence I scrounged up after proves he didn't do it. What I'm here to ask is whether you saw any strangers that day, in the hotel. Maybe back behind Slocum in the lobby, or on the steps."

A flicker of understanding passed over her face. "The upstairs steps?" she asked. "I mean, the ones to the second floor, not the outside ones?"

Kiefer nodded patiently. "Yes, ma'am. Those'd be the ones."

Her grip on the broom became less deathlike. "Well, as a matter of fact . . ." She pursed her lips and squinted, as if she were trying to recall.

"It's real important," interjected Josh, attempting to get back in the men's good graces.

"Hush," she said, shooting him a look that said he was still in the "seen but not heard" category so far as she was concerned, then said to Kiefer, "I believe so. I wasn't looking there at the moment the shot was fired, but just before, I did see a man standing at the base of the stairs, behind Mr. Slocum."

Slocum spoke for the first time. "Could you describe him, Mrs. Tinny?"

"Not well," she replied, although she said it to the sheriff, not Slocum. "He was a stranger to me. But he was wearing clothes with trail dust on them. I remember thinking that he was terribly dirty to come to a wedding! He was tall, but not as tall as Mr. Slocum. Perhaps about your height, Sheriff."

"Any scars?" Kiefer asked, visibly excited. "What color clothing? Or hair?"

"No, no scars that I recall," she said. "Rather pleasant looking in the face. Tan pants and a checkered shirt, I think. A red checkered shirt. And light brown hair. Sort of sandy colored. He was wearing a gun on his hip, but I didn't see it in his hand."

The sheriff doffed his hat. "Mrs. Tinny, I can't tell you how much help you've been. Thank you."

"I'll tell Frank that you called, Sheriff."

"Give him my regards. And by the way . . . have you seen this man anywhere else around town? Before or since the shooting?"

"Can't say that I have. But Sheriff?"

"Yes, ma'am?"

"When the shot was fired . . ." She smiled uncharacteristically. "Well, maybe it was just my imagination, but I remember thinking that it took a lot longer than it should have."

"Ma'am?"

"I'm probably being silly, but it seemed to me that there was some sort of echo to it. I mean, the report just seemed to go on for a very long time, even considering that he fired in a closed room." She shot Slocum a nasty look. "And I heard glass breaking,

too. Of course, that may have been someone drop-
ping his wineglass to the floor . . ."

Bill Messenger pushed back from the table at the
same café where he'd eaten the night before. He was
full of scrambled eggs and toast and ham and fried
potatoes, and he'd gotten them all at a reasonable
price. The crowd for breakfast had been somewhat
smaller than that the night before, and also merci-
fully less talkative. Nobody had said a word to him
except the waiter. He was grateful for this.

He stepped away from the table, nodded his
thanks to the waiter, then went outside. It was cool
for a June morning—which meant that it was
bearable—and he took up residence in a chair just
outside the front windows, in the shade. Up the street,
he had a good view of the hotel and the saloon.

He'd been watching them surreptitiously all morning. Lil was in there. He had mentally given himself
a good kicking already this morning, and more than
once. He should have snuck up to her room and finished the job last night, that was what.

But he hadn't, more's the pity. Now he was stuck
with doing it today, and with absolutely no plan in
mind. He was just going to watch until he saw her,
that was all. But he wasn't any too confident that he'd
think of the right move, even then.

It was just a pity he hadn't gotten her yesterday at
the wedding. Why did they have to shift at the last

second, anyway? He had rotten luck, that was why. He'd always had rotten luck. Something about Tiger Lil just brought it to the fore, that was all.

Well, screw her!

And then he found himself wishing that he had. Just once. Just one time, to make up for those years in prison, to make those work details in the beating sun and his tiny cell even halfway bearable. But he hadn't even had any fond memories to look back on.

Which was another reason she deserved to die like the bitch she was.

He dug into one of his pockets and pulled out his whittling knife, then ferreted in another to find the bit of pine he'd been working on. It was slowly taking form as a tiny pronghorn antelope. Messenger had been quite the woodcarver back in the days before he went away to Yuma. He wasn't up to his old skills yet, though. He figured it would just take time.

And he was patient.

Look how long he'd waited to get back at Lil!

He started whittling his little pronghorn, glancing up the street every few seconds. Besides Lil, he had another problem: how to flee Poleaxe once he'd accomplished the deed. He didn't own a horse, and he'd used up practically all his cash on the stage, just to get here.

He supposed he could always steal one, but dammit, he wouldn't want to go through all this crud to get back at Lil, only to be hanged for thieving a horse!

He stilled his fingers. He'd nearly cut off one of the pronghorn's legs, which he most surely didn't want to do. He sat there for a moment, very still, and thinking, *Just calm the hell down, Bill! Something will happen. It always does, doesn't it?*

Slocum stood in the lobby while Lil settled her account, and the desk clerk made over her, offering his sympathies over and over on the untimely death of her husband and offering, at the same time, his hopes that she'd had a pleasant stay. Slocum was embarrassed for him, but Lil didn't seem to mind.

The thought of all that land and money she'd just come into probably made up for a lot of indiscretions on the part of the townspeople.

She had mentioned that David Chandler's attorney had come to see her early this morning. She hadn't seemed a bit sad about it, either.

Apparently, she got everything. And there was a lot of everything to get.

"Ready, Lil?" he asked when she turned away from the desk.

"I believe I am, Slocum," she said, and hoisting his bedroll under his arm to fill his hands with most of her luggage, he led her through the front door.

The livery had sent up a buckboard—nothing fancy—to take them out to her ranch, and the desk clerk followed behind them, dragging her big trunk. Once they got it loaded to Slocum's satisfaction, he checked his Appy's tether line, then climbed up into the driver's seat beside Lil.

He gave a cluck to the horses, and a little shake of the reins, and they were off. As they drove down Main Street, he noticed a fellow sitting out front of the café, a man just sitting there, whittling, but who looked up and watched their progress with some interest.

It might have been a local, just snooping on them to have a good story to tell later on, at the bar. Then again, it might be a suspect. Slocum thought he recognized him, maybe from dinner last night. It was hard to tell at this distance. And he didn't want to actually turn back at stare at the fellow. Why alert him if he was, indeed, important?

"I'm gettin' spooky in my old age," he muttered.

And Lil asked, "What did you say?"

"Nothin', darlin'," he replied, letting a smile spread out over his face. "Nothin' at all."

19

She had warmed up quite a bit since they'd come to question her the morning before. Not enough for her to lean against his side as he drove. Not enough for her to pepper his cheek with kisses or slide her hand up his thigh. But enough that once they reached the ranch, she thought she just might have him do some more . . . *domestic* work, rather than fixing fences.

Something that could be best accomplished in the bedroom.

"You ever been out here, Lil?" Slocum asked.

"No, David never showed me the ranch," she said. "I guess he was saving it for a surprise." She hoped it would be a big, fat, juicy surprise. Something like a jewel of a house, set amid green lawns and . . .

And then she remembered she was in Arizona. Just a rough house set in the middle of the gravelly desert would probably be more like it.

"Hope so," Slocum muttered, and Lil knew he'd been thinking much the same as she. She smiled.

Not long after Slocum and Lil left town on the buckboard, Bill Messenger took a leisurely stroll down to the livery and rented himself a horse for the day. He set off, following the telltale ruts of the buckboard's passing, but he didn't hurry. There was plenty of time. Besides, at his current slow jog, he'd catch up with that buckboard before it got halfway to the ranch.

He hadn't asked the man at the livery about this, though. Best not to raise suspicions. He'd gotten it out of a local over dinner last night.

The horse he'd rented was just that: a sorrel, broken-down rental horse, with choppy gaits and all. Probably twenty years old, too. Didn't neck rein worth spit, and he was pretty certain that the gelding was deaf, too. At least, Jess, back at the livery, had shouted directly into its ear every time he wanted it to do something.

Like get the hell off his foot, for instance.

It seemed to be the beast's favorite place to stand.

Well, Messenger wouldn't have to worry about that. All he needed was some halfway reliable transportation to take him to Lil. That, and a loaded gun.

And now he had both.

He wasn't sure just exactly how much trouble this Slocum character would be, but he'd done time with some god-awful rowdies, and he figured he was prepared for the worst. The very worst. He could handle it.

He was about a mile out of town when he began to have doubts. Mainly because his halfway reliable transportation suddenly stumbled—over his own feet was the only thing Messenger could figure——and pulled up lame.

Messenger dismounted and checked the hoof, cleaned it out, looking for stones, and even felt the whole of the pastern and lower leg, feeling for heat.

He couldn't find an injury, couldn't even find a clue.

And the gelding still limped when he led it a few feet.

Damn it!

Charlie Townsend was up and around, too.

His shoulder hurt him some less this morning, although he found out real quick that you didn't want to do something foolish, like reach up to the top shelf for coffee.

He could have grabbed it with his good side, but instead he went without his own brew and wandered down to the bunkhouse to grab a cup of Cookie's, instead.

His face was looking pretty damned good, too. If he squinted into the mirror really hard, he could just make out, just faintly, a few dim, pink lines where the glass had scratched him. But he figured a fellow would have to look long and hard to find them.

All in all, he was pretty chipper.

Some might say, a lot more chipper than a man who had just committed one murder and was about to commit another had any right to look. Charlie, how-

ever, wasn't one of those unnamed "some" and didn't
give it a second thought. After partaking of the bunkhouse coffee and handing out orders for the day, he
went back to his little cottage and sat on the porch,
cleaning his guns.

And whistling.

He felt damned good this morning.

He hadn't been at it too long when he saw a buckboard approaching, far out on the road, from the direction of town. From long habit, he quickly
reassembled the gun he'd been cleaning, slid five
shiny new bullets into the cylinder, and clicked it
closed with a sharp snap.

Only then did he stand up to take a closer look.

The buckboard—he'd been right about that part,
anyhow—wasn't much closer, but close enough that
he could see there was an Appy saddle horse tied to
and being led by the back rail of it, and two people on
the front seat.

A man and a woman.

A scowl gripped him from head to toe in a way it
never had. It was that woman! That woman, come to
take his ranch!

Anger froze him solid, or he would have grabbed
his rifle and taken a shot at her from where he stood.
It was a good thing that anger prevailed, because he
realized a mere second later that this would have
been the worst move he could possibly have made.
First off, there were too many people around, and
him in plain sight of most all of them!

He'd need to be plenty tricky to pull this off.

At last, he managed to thaw out his muscles, holster his gun, and take a stiff walk off the porch and out into the yard to greet the buckboard—and its inhabitants.

The man, Slocum, gave him a curious look when he stepped down, but shook his hand and said, "So you're Chandler's foreman. Pleased to meet you."

That damn floozy, Lil, said just about the same thing. Oh, she was pretty, all right, a real treat to the eyes, but she wasn't going to fool him the way she'd fooled nearly every man in the whole territory.

Why, one of the hands—a new kid named Thad Turner—fainted dead away! Charlie figured it'd be years before the rest of the boys got done teasing Thad about that!

Charlie gave orders for some of the men to follow them with Lil's baggage, then led Lil and Slocum to the house. He knew it was silly, but he couldn't get over the feeling that Slocum was looking at him funny, like he had the smallpox or something.

He brushed aside the feeling, though, and opened the front door, ushering them inside.

"This here's the parlor," he said, then swung his arm over to the side. "Kitchen's in there. Dinin' room, too."

"The bedrooms are back here?" asked Lil. She was already at the mouth of the hall. Just like a woman!

Anger this time took the form of bile rising to the

back of his throat. But he nodded and managed to say, "Yes, ma'am. Three of 'em."

She smiled and said, "Good. Then there'll be plenty of room for you to stay in the house, Mr. Slocum. Mr. Townsend, Sheriff Kiefer has asked Slocum to be my bodyguard for a few days."

Charlie swallowed hard to clear his throat and said, "Yes, ma'am."

The men began to traipse through the front door with Lil's trunks, and she disappeared down the hall, obviously in search of the best room. Which left Slocum and Charlie standing uncomfortably in the parlor.

Charlie couldn't stand it any longer. He said, "Mr. Slocum, seems you're looking at me kinda odd. Any particular reason for that?"

Slocum's features took on the very image of innocence. "Kind of odd? Nope, don't think so, unless it's just my natural vacant expression." He put a hand on the shoulder of a passing ranch hand, pointed to the saddlebags and bedroll the man was carrying, and said, "You can just leave those with me, son."

The hand did as he was told, but lingered. "Are you him? I mean, are you the Slocum they write about, mister?"

Slocum seemed to take a long breath. "I am," he finally said, "but don't take anything you read to heart. They make most of that shit up." And then he smiled and winked.

"Th-thank you," the hand stuttered, wide-eyed,

and backed nearly to the front door before he turned, went outside, and from the porch, shouted, "Hey you, Curly! You owe me a sawbuck!"

"You *are* the one in them books," Charlie Townsend said flatly. Slocum didn't quite know how to take the comment, considering the manner in which it was said, so he just nodded curtly.

"I read one'a those," Charlie continued. "One a while back."

Again, Slocum just nodded.

Charlie shifted his weight. His eyes narrowed. "You make much'a anything off those?"

Slocum smiled. "You thinkin' of going into the dime hero business?"

"Just curious, that's all."

"Well, the answer is no. I don't make a plug nickel off 'em. The writer does, I suppose," he added when Charlie's weathered face fell. "And the folks who publish 'em. Me, I'm just a . . . a topic, I guess you'd call it."

"You mean they can use your name and not pay you for it?" Charlie asked. He appeared to be more than a little incensed on Slocum's behalf.

"Reckon so. They're doin' it."

"Don't seem fair," Charlie huffed. "Don't even seem American!"

Slocum shrugged, said, "That's the way it is," and hoped Lil would reappear damn soon.

He had the foggiest recollection of having seen

Charlie somewhere before, and the association it was bringing up was none too good. He just wished he could remember!

The hands, minus the luggage they'd traipsed in with, began to emerge from the hall right about then, thus effectively shutting Charlie's piehole. For the moment. Slocum nodded and said his thanks to each man as he passed, and when the last one let the screen door slam behind him, Charlie set in again.

"Them things they write about you. You say they make most of 'em up?"

He was like a dog with a bone, Charlie was. Slocum said, "'Fraid so. Parts of 'em are true, though, if you take 'em with a grain of salt."

"Which parts?"

Slocum exhaled loudly. "Charlie, that's like tryin' to pick the black pepper outta the fly shit. Let's just leave it at some here, some there."

Charlie nodded sagely and said, "I reckon so." But then he brightened. "That big leopard Appy tied behind the buckboard. He's yours, ain't he?"

Slocum nodded. "That part's true."

"Well, then," Charlie said, seemingly satisfied. "Well, then."

Just then, Lil's bright, "Slocum?" wafted up the hall, and he had his excuse.

Shrugging, he said, "Duty calls, I reckon. See you later, Charlie."

* * *

Lil waited in the largest bedroom, her trunk and bags scattered about the room. She heard Slocum's boot steps coming down the hall, and a little shiver ran up her spine. Gone was her desire to send Slocum out to the fields and the fences, gone was any wish except to have him right here and right now, deep inside her.

As his steps drew closer, her fingers flew to the buttons of her bodice, and by the time he entered the room, hat in his hand, she had unbuttoned it to the waist and was already working at the ties of her chemise.

Slocum cocked a brow.

"You a little anxious, Lil?"

She snorted. "As if you're not. I know you too well, Slocum."

"I reckon you do," he said, suddenly sweeping her off her feet and into his arms. "But not good enough to know I won't make love to you in your dead husband's bedroom."

He carried her out into the hall and to one of the smaller rooms, tossed her on the bed, and lifted her skirts.

For a moment, she couldn't see for the cloud of taffeta in her face, but she could certainly feel it when he parted her thighs and pushed deep inside her, filling her completely. Batting her hems away from her face, she let out a satisfied sigh and lifted her legs, wrapping them around his hips. Her arms ringed his neck.

"That's my boy," she murmured.

"That's my girl," he said with a grin and began to move inside her.

He was wonderful, as always. He fit her, and she him, as if they had been made for each other.

She tingled when he pushed her camisole aside to expose one breast, and shivered with pleasure when he fastened his mouth on her nipple and began to tease it with his teeth. She tried to push everything— her pelvis, her breast, her face—up toward him, to meet him, to merge with him, to be one with the thrusting, powerful force of him.

Why couldn't he have money? she wondered, even as she lost herself in him. Slocum was the one man on earth that she could have stayed with, lived with, and loved forever. But a saddle tramp was always a saddle tramp—which meant no visible means of support—and it was hard to soothe itchy feet.

And then his hands slipped between her fanny and the fabric of her skirt. They cupped her and lifted her, pulling her hard against him over and over, until she found herself tumbling, tumbling, tumbling into a teeth-clenching, molar-grinding, lose-your-mind orgasm that seemed to go on forever.

She felt him spasm as he came inside her, and if her eyes had been open, she knew she would have seen the telltale grimace of ultimate satisfaction he always made just as the sensation overtook him.

He pumped into her once more, then twice, before

he relaxed and collapsed next to her on the coverlet and pulled her atop him.

"God damn you, girl!" he said, head back, eyes closed, and a little out of breath. "I'm so mad at you, I could just spank you."

20

Bill Messenger, now afoot and leading his limping gelding, drew slowly closer to the Circle C.

And with every step he took, he plotted his revenge against the fair Lil.

Shooting was really too good for her, although he couldn't think of anything more expedient or anything that could be accomplished from farther away.

After all, she had stolen not only his money and his past but his future as well. She'd stolen his whole life, when you came right down to it, and it probably hadn't bothered her as much as a sneeze.

The closer he got, that madder he got, until, within sight of the ranch, he had to stop just to calm himself down.

"Get a grip, Bill," he muttered. "Just cool yourself down, dammit. If you go in there hot under the collar, you're not gonna get anybody killed but yourself."

It was good advice, and he took it.

He stood there a good, long time, baking in the noonday sun, before he started forward again.

* * *

"Spank me?" Lil lifted her head and rolled right off Slocum, pushing down her skirts and pulling her bodice closed. "Why on earth?"

Slocum didn't move. Calmly, he said, "First, you make a whole bunch of people so mad that they want to kill you. Second, you somehow manage to get your 'husband' killed in your place. You let the sheriff arrest me, you break me out of jail at gunpoint, and then you spill your guts to him at the drop of a hat and expect me to make love to you at your whim. That about answer your question?"

She let that lay there for a second before she murmured, "Wasn't it good for you?"

He rolled toward her so quickly that she jumped, and he growled, "That ain't the point, honey."

Charlie Townsend had a plan.

He'd decided the best time to do it would be at night, after everybody was asleep.

Now, his little house was set at a right angle to the big place. There weren't any doors on the side that would block any vantage point from the bunkhouse, but that was all right, he figured. He'd leave a window open.

He could sneak out the front, go down the side of the big house to Chandler's bedroom—where that bitch had undoubtedly camped out, seeing as how it was the biggest and best—shoot her through her window as she slept, then sprint back to his cottage and jump through his bedroom window before anybody got past the bunkhouse door to see what the noise was about.

It was a very fine plan, and he congratulated himself on coming up with it.

He'd even gone so far as to test the ground between the two houses, to see if it would hold a print. What he found was that the little patch of ground was already rife with footprints—both horse and human, and a few goat tracks. Nobody'd be able to make head nor tail of his passing.

He even made a test run at jumping through his bedroom window, after making certain that nobody was watching.

Easy as pie.

At the moment, he was down at the barn, helping Ron shoe a couple of horses. He kept his face passive and his hands on his work, and every time somebody mentioned the woman up at the big house, he just smiled and agreed that yes, she sure was a looker.

Nobody would suspect him.

Not in a million years.

In Poleaxe, Sheriff Kiefer had been walking and talking with Chance Moody and thinking all the while about the murder.

A third shooter. There had to have been a third shooter. Mrs. Tinny, the mayor's wife, would attest to it, but she was only one witness, and a woman at that.

He was afraid that her testimony wouldn't hold much water in front of a male jury. Especially one which, to a man, had all liked David Chandler.

He and Chance said their good-byes, and Kiefer found himself down at the edge of town, near the livery. Might as well drop in and pass some time with Jess. There'd been a passel of strangers in town over the past week, but maybe Jess had seen one fellow more suspicious than the rest.

He didn't have much hope, but he headed toward the livery, anyway.

"Jess?" he shouted when he stuck his head in the door. "You around?"

From behind the flimsy door of his sleeping room, Jess's voice shouted, "Keep your shirt on!"

Kiefer smiled. "It's just Miles Kiefer, Jess. Sorry to disturb you, if you were workin' on something."

Working on catching up on next month's sleep if he knew Jess, Kiefer thought.

But in a moment, Jess opened the door and stepped out into the barn. "No trouble, Sheriff, no trouble at all." He smoothed his hair—what there was of it—with a hand. "What you need?"

Miles leaned against a stall's wall, hooking his elbow over the top of the corner post. "Just wanted to ask, Jess, if you've had any folks through here in the past few days that you thought looked suspicious."

"Sure have!" the stableman answered quickly. "That Slocum feller! Why, he was right suspicious, if you was to ask me, which you happen to be doin'. Always thought so."

Kiefer stifled his grin and said, "Besides him, I mean, Jess. Anybody odd?"

Jess thinned his lips into a long, straight line and slowly shook his head. "Nope. Not that I recamember. Sorry. Always like to help the law when I can, Sheriff."

Kiefer nodded. "I know that, Jess, and I'm obliged to you."

"So why'd you let that murderous Slocum out of jail, Miles? He come in here this morning and rented hisself a buckboard, and took his own horse along, too."

"Know he did, Jess," Kiefer replied. "It's a long story."

Jess sat down on a straw bale and made himself comfortable. "I got time."

Aw, hell, thought Kiefer. But he had time on his hands, too, so he started to tell the story.

"Miz Chandler?" shouted a voice from the parlor. "Miz Chandler? Mr. Slocum?"

"Shit," Slocum muttered and sat straight up, abandoning Lil midconversation. "What?" he hollered back, even as he quicky buttoned his pants and ran the back of his hand over his mouth, in case Lil had smeared any lip rouge on him.

He stuck his head out into the hall. Sure enough,

there was one of the younger hands, standing smack in the center of the parlor and twisting his hat in his fingers.

"Don't anybody knock anymore?" Slocum asked.

It must have come out gruffer than he intended, because the boy shrank visibly and muttered, "Sorry, sir. Right sorry."

Slocum said, "It's all right. What can I do for you?"

"Just wondered if you might need any help, is all," the boy answered. "You know, unpackin' or gettin' settled in."

"What's your name?"

"Curly, Mr. Slocum. Curly Jamison."

Slocum guessed this was the same Curly that had lost the bet with the other hand. He didn't bother to ask, though.

"No thanks, we're gettin' along just fine in here, Curly. But thanks for thinkin' about it."

Curly seemed disappointed but nodded. "Yessir, just thought I'd make myself useful iff'n I could." He planted his hat back on his head and dragged himself out of the house like he was going to his own funeral.

"You should have let him do something," said Lil from behind him. He turned to find her buttoned into the top of her dress again, with her skirts pulled firmly down around her ankles. "Boys like that . . . Idol worship and all . . ."

"Idol worship?" he asked, puzzled. He could see a

kid like that worshiping Lil, all right, but he would have called it something different.

Lil seemed to know what he was thinking, because she said, "No, silly. You're the one he worships. Why, I saw at least three of those Slocum books tucked into as many back pockets when we rode in!"

Slocum sat down, rather suddenly, in a wooden chair beside the door.

Kiefer ran himself out of steam—and out of story—and he said, "That's it, Jess. All I got the air for, anyway."

Jess pursed his lips for a second, then said, "Well I'll be double-dogged. Just plain double-dogged. Three fellers, not one!"

Kiefer nodded. "So anything you saw, or noticed, or even thought was a little out of the ordinary, Jess. It'd be a big help."

Jess scratched the back of his wattly neck. "Well, now, come to think of it, there was somethin'. But it didn't happen until today, so likely, it don't matter."

Kiefer was of the same opinion, but asked Jess to go on, just to be polite. Also, it meant that much less time he'd have to spend in his office, staring at the wall and calling himself an idiot.

"Feller came in here this forenoon—about an hour after Slocum come in and rented my buckboard," he said. "Wouldn't've thought nothin' of it, 'cept he said he didn't have much cash, and could I rent him a horse for a quarter."

Kiefer's eyes narrowed.

"So, I took pity on him and said he could take old Rufus. You know my Rufus, Miles?"

Kiefer nodded. "Miracle he made it out of his stall, Jess. There ought to be a law against renting out Rufus."

"Yup. There ain't, though," Jess said, almost defiantly. "You want I should go on?"

Kiefer nodded impatiently.

"But the feller looked him over and took me up on it, so I slung a saddle and bridle on him—free of charge—and handed him over. Danged horse goes lame every fifteen minutes. Can't figure why that feller ain't led him back in here already."

"What'd this boy look like, Jess?"

"Hell, you know what he looks like, Miles! Sorrel with a stripe down his face and two white socks in front and one in back, and—"

Kiefer held up a hand. "Not Rufus, Jess. The feller that rented him."

Jess nodded. "Oh, him. Nice enough lookin' feller. Kinda sandy-colored hair. Taller than most. Dressed kinda cheap. I mean, I didn't have no trouble believin' that he was down on his luck, if you know what I mean."

"Which way did he head?"

Jess had a scratch again while he thought this over.

"Out south," he finally said. "Just like he was trailin' that buckboard Slocum took out earlier."

Kiefer uncurled his elbow from the stall's post, peeled his back from the stall's wall, stood up straight, and said, "Thanks, Jess. You've been a big help."

"Glad to be of service, Miles, dang glad. You want I should get your mount ready? You gonna take off after that feller?" Jess was on his feet, too.

"No, I . . ." Kiefer thought again. The lead wasn't much, but it was more than he'd had before. And the thought of going back to the office didn't exactly sit right with him.

So he thumbed his hat back on his head, and he said, "Yeah, Jess. Why don't you saddle up my horse? Believe I'll take a little ride out toward the Circle C."

Jess hurried toward the third stall from the right.

I'm batty, Kiefer thought to himself as he rode out of town at a slow jog. *I've gone clear round the bend, and I'm not going to find a thing out here except some poor lunatic leading a lame horse toward me.*

Still, it was better than the silence that awaited him in his office.

How could he be expected to ferret out the man who had done the real killing when the whole town was full of strangers, when nobody had seen a thing but Mrs. Tinny? And she hadn't really seen

much at all, had she? Just "a man" standing behind
Slocum.

Even Slocum hadn't seen anything.

For not the first time, Kiefer considered arresting
Slocum all over again. It would shut a whole lot of
people up, anyway.

But something inside him wouldn't let him do it.
There was all that broken glass, busted through from
the inside, and then there was that slug he'd dug out
of the wall of the mercantile this morning, the slug he
still carried in his pocket.

He reminded himself to go check the walls of the
hotel lobby for another slug. If the man at the window hadn't hit Chandler, he had to have hit something. Most likely, a wall.

Sometimes, Kiefer really hated his job.

This was one of those times.

He figured that all he was doing was trying to sort
out various devils, and what kind of a job was that,
unless you were a preacher? He'd known Chandler
wasn't on the up and up. He knew that Slocum was a
celebrated shootist. Tiger Lil herself wasn't exactly
an angel, if Slocum were to be believed. And whoever the man at the window had been—and the man
behind Slocum, whose slug had really hit
Chandler—they weren't exactly a pair of do-gooders,
either.

He shook his head. Some kind of a job he had, all
right!

21

Outside, in the barn, Slocum was checking on his horse. The gelding had been fed, as he requested, but not rubbed down to his standards.

He found a curry comb and a body brush and set to work on the leopard Appy.

He always did a lot of thinking while he was grooming his horse, and a great deal of problem solving. But this day brought him more questions than answers. Damn that Lily, anyway! And damn him!

Why had he felt so goddamned compelled to follow her trail into Poleaxe? Well, that was really a rhetorical question, wasn't it? Like a hound dog, his nose was always to the ground, sniffing out the nearest bitch in heat.

But, Lord, what a mess they'd made this time! Why hadn't he decided to skip the wedding? Why hadn't he gone over to the saloon instead, or down to the livery, or just stayed in his room?

The point was moot. He hadn't done any of those things. He'd done what he had, and what he seemed to do best; be in the worst possible place at the worst possible moment.

Having finished the horse's right side, he walked

round the backside and started on the left. He was down the neck and working diligently on the shoulder when he raised his head at the sound of someone leading a horse into the barn.

He squinted. "Didn't I eat supper with you the other night? Over to the café?"

The man, whose mount was limping badly, looked right back at him and said, "Could be. I ate there."

Slocum turned his attention back to the Appy's shoulder. "Nice to see you again. Did you work for Chandler?"

The man, who had passed him and was presently tying his mount to a post in the barn, hesitated before he said, "Nope. I was just wonderin' if they might need more help. I heard about Mr. Chandler. That was sure a sorry business."

The man bent and lifted his horse's hoof.

"It sure was," replied Slocum.

"I can't figure out what's makin' this horse so lame!" the man said in exasperation. "No rocks have cut or bruised him, his tendon's not bowed . . ."

Slocum set aside his brushes and strolled over. He took the horse's hoof from the man. "Here, lemme see." He studied on the hoof for a good, long time, squinting at it, then pointed with his index finger. "There," he said. "Hairline crack in the wall."

"Figures!" spat the newcomer. "That old joker at the livery cheated me! I swear, seems that if it weren't for bad luck, I wouldn't have no luck at all."

"I hear you, pal," Slocum said and put down the

horse's hoof again. "I think that Jess at the livery is smarter than he looks."

The stranger stood up straight and scowled. "And that means what? That I'm dumber?"

Slocum shrugged. "Didn't mean nothin' by it, pal. If you're lookin' for a job, you go round to that little house past the big one. Foreman lives there, name's Townsend. Charlie Townsend."

The man nodded his thanks and started out toward the yard.

Almost as an afterthought, Slocum called, "What's your name again, mister?"

"Bill Messenger," came the answer. And then he was gone. He didn't ask Slocum's name. Slocum thought that was a little funny, but just then he happened into a concentrated patch of dirt on the Appy's belly, and it distracted him.

He did not, in fact, recall the conversaton until some time later.

Lil sat on her new bed amid her open trunks and valises and grinned like a fool.

Oh, she'd really fallen into the cream this time! She been through all of David's bureau drawers, and found countless goodies: gold nugget cufflinks, two diamond stickpins; a tissue-wrapped, ivory and silver dresser set, which must have been his mother's by the initials engraved on them; and hidden at the back of his handkerchief drawer, a beautiful jade necklace, carved in the shape of a dragon, and earrings to match. They must have been squirreled away for him to give her later on.

The furnishings were all expensive, even lavish. She hadn't been through the desk in the parlor yet, but there was time for that, plenty of time. His bankbook would be there, she figured, as well as any deeds or important papers he'd had.

She had, she reminded herself.

She let out a giggle.

Life was not only good, it was, quite frankly, amazing!

And she had Slocum to boot!

Oh, not forever. She wasn't anybody's fool, and she knew that *nothing* about Slocum was forever. But she had him for a time, and she had him all to herself, with no distractions like saloons or poker games or horse races to get in the way.

She giggled again and hugged herself.

This might very well be the last time she would play the game. If David had been as rich as she thought, she could sell out, move to San Francisco, and live the life of Riley for the rest of her days.

She had bank accounts all over the place, didn't she? Those, combined with all this, must be worth eight or nine hundred thousand. Maybe a million.

It was just too bad about Slocum. She wouldn't have minded supporting him for a time, not really, although it would probably grow old in a hurry. And then she'd begin to resent him, and he her, and . . .

No, it was better just to take him as he was, and for as long as he wanted to stay, and leave it at that.

Besides, Slocum likely wouldn't stand for any woman paying his bills!

She rose and wandered to the window and looked, at a sharp angle, toward the front of the house, to the little slice of barnyard she could see next to the caretaker's cottage. She hoped to catch a glimpse of Slocum out there, doing whatever men did on ranches.

But instead she saw someone else. Someone who made her breath catch in her throat, and not in a good way, either.

She just saw him as he disappeared into the foreman's front door, and he was dressed much more poorly than she could ever have imagined, but she knew him.

"Bill . . ." she whispered, and her knees gave way beneath her.

Bill Messenger pulled out a chair at the foreman's insistence and sat himself down. The man facing him was a salty old hand, crusted over by years of hard work and burnt and dappled by the sun.

"So, you're lookin' for work, Messenger," said Charlie Townsend as he settled his bony frame into the chair. "You got any experience?"

Experience? He'd built a ranching empire out of nothing, commanded men, bred cattle and horses, and owned a saloon. But he said, "Done some bronc bustin'. Cattle work, too. Ropin' and brandin' and the like."

"You work anywhere I would'a heard of?"

"Not unless you spent a lot of time up in Montana or Colorado, Mr. Townsend."

The man grunted. "Call me Charlie. Everybody does."

"All right, Charlie."

"You mind mendin' fences, paintin' 'em, that sort of deal?"

"No sir. I just want some work. I ain't picky." Now that was the truth, wasn't it? And he especially wanted to work right here. Outside, he could hear men hitching up the buckboard again, likely to take it back to town. He said, "You got any fellers headed back to town anytime today? That's a rented horse I got out there, and he's lame to boot. Like to get him back to the livery."

Surprisingly, Charlie smiled. He said, "Jess rent you Rufus?"

Messenger scowled. "I believe that was the name he said, yes."

Then Charlie broke out in a laugh—an insulting sort of laugh, if you asked Messenger.

"Hell, that nag's got to be thirty if he's a day!" Charlie said between gales of laughter. "That Jess! He's a caution, all right!"

Messenger simply sat there, gripping the arms of his chair. At last, he asked, "Am I hired?"

"Well, Messenger," Townsend said, wiping his eyes, "you're in luck. We've got a band of two-year-olds comin' in from the S Bar S. Expectin' 'em tomorrow or the next day. They'll need to be broke, all right. Expect most of 'em are pretty green."

"Fine by me," said Messenger, and he stood up. Charlie rose along with him. "Oh. How much does it pay?"

"Thirty dollars a month and found," Charlie said quickly and moved to the door to let him out. "See them fellers with the buckboard?" he asked. "Hand over Rufus to them. They'll take him in to Jess at the livery."

"Right kind," said Messenger and tipped his hat. He walked out onto the porch, and over his shoulder, Charlie called, "Hey, Curly! This here is Bill Messenger. New bronc buster. Take Rufus back to town for him, would you?"

Curly, a lean man with tightly curled red hair, shook his head and laughed. "Rufus? He lamed up again? That dang Jess!"

Messenger shrugged and walked on, out past the wagon and into the barn to reclaim the hapless Rufus.

22

Lil was in a panic.

Bill was out there. He'd ruin everything. He was probably the one who had shot at her. Suddenly, everything that Slocum and the sheriff had said made sense to her, where it had been just babble before.

It *was* her that the gunman had been after. And the gunman was Bill. Her husband.

Former husband.

No, husband. One of them.

She'd lost count, really.

The first thing she'd done when she ducked back away from the window was to grab a small bag filled with feather boas, dump it out, and proceed to hurriedly pack it with just the things she'd need to survive.

But now that it was packed, she sat on the bed, staring first at it, then all the nice furniture around her, and the paintings, and thinking about what was in that desk in the front room . . .

And she knew she couldn't leave. Not now. Not at this stage of the game. Not with all these goodies, newly won, and at great expense. Mostly David's, but that was beside the point.

Maybe she could provoke Slocum into shooting Bill! That would solve all her problems, wouldn't it?

But it would most certainly bring up a few new ones for Slocum. No, she couldn't use him in that way. She'd caused him enough trouble already, poor darling.

However, she had no such compunctions about using one of the other men.

But who? Not that Charlie, the ranch foreman. He was too old, and Bill would probably kill him. One of the younger boys? That should probably be avoided, too. Bill was pretty good with a firearm, as she recalled.

Maybe she should take care of it herself.

But how?

She'd have to think on it, because it had to be perfect. No lose ends.

Quietly, efficiently, her devious little mind began to turn its wheels and mesh its gears.

She must have been sitting there for an hour when Slocum's call brought her to her senses.

"Lil! Lily! You hungry?" he shouted from the front of the house, and she suddenly realized that something smelled awfully good.

He'd cooked! How lovely!

"Coming, Slocum!" she called in her sweetest voice. She hadn't come up with a plan yet—or a dupe to pull it off—and she might still have to fall back on Slocum. She'd best be as accommodating as possible.

She slid her shoes back on, set her packed bag aside, and went up the hall.

He had, indeed, been cooking. She could have told that by the mess in the kitchen, even if her sense of smell had disappeared. But lucky for her—and for Slocum—it had done no such thing.

The table was set with a pan of enchiladas, smothered in cheese, a bowl of crispy pan-fried potatoes, a basket of fluffy biscuits with butter and honey, a steaming bowl of peas, and another, bigger bowl of savory beef stew.

The meal didn't exactly match itself, all things considered, but he'd really tried, and she had to give him credit. As a matter of fact, she was seriously touched by the effort.

"Slocum!" she gasped. "I'm amazed! Did you do this all by yourself?"

He was leaning in the kitchen doorway, and he smiled. "Self-defense, Lil. I've had your cookin' before."

"Oh, you!" she snarled—but was careful to keep it playful.

She walked into the dining room, and so did he, and he pulled out a chair for her.

"Just campfire cookin', only over a stove instead of an open fire," he said as he seated himself. He didn't stand on ceremony. He grabbed the pan of enchiladas straight off and scooped three of them onto his plate. As an afterthought, he passed them to Lil, who served herself one.

After all, if he was eating three, they were probably all right. In fact, they both helped themselves to everything on the table. Lil enjoyed the meal all the more because she'd skipped lunch. They both had, as shown by the size of Slocum's servings.

Once the edge was off her hunger, her mind wandered back to more pressing things. Bill Messenger, for instance. Should she tell Slocum about him? She really didn't want to, not at all, but she hadn't yet come up with a satisfactory alternative. She was about to open her mouth, to start a conversation headed in that general direction, when somebody knocked at the door.

She excused herself and went to answer it, vetoing Slocum's idea of just hollering, "Come in!"

And she opened it to find the sheriff.

Her head cocked in surprise, she said, "Hello, Sheriff. Won't you come in? We were just having some dinner. I'll set an extra place if you—"

"No, thank you, ma'am," he said as he crossed the threshhold and took off his hat. He looked toward the bounty on the dining room table and at Slocum— who waved, because his mouth was full—and said, "Somethin' sure smells mighty good though."

She smiled, "Slocum says it's just campfire cooking over a real stove, but I think he's an artist."

In the dining room, Slocum snorted.

"I wonder, Mrs. Chandler, if I could borrow Slocum for a minute?"

She didn't answer for a moment. What did he want? Why had he ridden all the way out here, and at sunset, too?

She heard Slocum's chair scrape back, and hurriedly, she said, "Certainly, Sheriff."

When he arrived, she didn't budge.

Napkin in hand, he asked, "What is it, Kiefer?"

"Passed your buckboard comin' out," Kiefer said. "There was a saddle horse tied to it."

"And?" said Slocum.

"Who rode in on it?"

"New hand, I guess," Slocum said. "Least, I sent him over to see Charlie Townsend. Must've got hired if he sent his mount back to town."

"Know where he is?"

"Townsend? He's back at his house, I reckon."

The sheriff turned to Lil. "Like to talk to him, ma'am, if I could."

Lil's insides were twisting into a knot, but very calmly, she said, "Of course! Why ask me?"

Kiefer nodded, his mouth quirking up into a slightly amused grin, and said, "It's your place, now."

"Oh," she said, a little embarrassed. "I suppose it is . . ."

Slocum saw the sheriff out, while she stood there,

confused. If the sheriff wanted to talk to her foreman about Bill Messenger, that must mean he was onto something. But what that something was, she couldn't figure out.

Slocum stepped out on the porch with Kiefer and shut the door behind them. "What have you got?"

Kiefer shrugged. "Not much, but I figured it was better than nothing. You know old Jess, down at the livery?"

"Yeah?"

"He told me about this galoot. Thought he was actin' strange."

Slocum smirked and said, "Jess oughta know."

Kiefer smiled. "Well, there is that . . ." He rubbed the back of his neck. "Anyway, figured to talk to Charlie first, then have a little chat with Mr. Messenger."

"Messenger?"

"Fella that rented the horse."

With that, Miles stepped down off the porch and headed for the caretaker's cottage, leaving Slocum to wonder about Messenger.

"Don't know anything much than what I already told you," replied Townsend. In the gathering darkness, he and the sheriff stood on the porch. He hadn't invited Kiefer in.

"Nothing?" Kiefer pressed. "You'd hire a man with no more reference than that?"

"Got broncs comin' in." Townsend shrugged. "Gotta get 'em broke."

Kiefer tugged his hat brim. "You mind if I go find him and talk to him?"

Townsend shrugged again, although this time, theatrically. "Don't make me no never mind." His brow furrowed. "What you want with him, anyhow?"

"Nothing," Kiefer answered, trying to keep things casual. "I just thought he might have seen something. You know, the other day."

"Seen something about Slocum killin' Mr. Chandler?"

"Thought you'd already been told, Charlie," Kiefer said. "Slocum didn't kill Chandler. All he killed was some glass."

At Charlie's puzzled expression, Kiefer added, "Shot out the window."

"Why'd anybody want to do that?"

"To stop the fella who was outside the window, aiming at Mr. Chandler," Kiefer said, nearing exasperation.

That stopped Charlie cold. Finally, he said, "Try the bunkhouse."

"Will do," said Kiefer with a quick nod. "Thanks."

"Any time, Sheriff," Charlie replied and was inside and behind the closed door before Miles even had a chance to step off the porch.

And as he walked toward the bunkhouse, he wondered what on earth had put the burr under Charlie's blanket.

He waved a hand at one of the boys as he walked through the open bunkhouse door. Cookie was hard at work, stirring up pot of something—probably vile—on the old stove. "Howdy, boys," he said in reply to the shouted greetings from several of the men.

He looked around but didn't spot his man, so he put a hand on the shoulder of the closest cowboy. "Curly, you know Bill Messenger?"

"The new man?"

"Yes."

"He's right over there," Curly said, and pointed toward a lone man in the corner. "What you want him for?"

"Questioning. Might be a witness to a crime."

Curly nodded. "Oh. Go ahead, I guess," he said, as if the likes of Curly could prevent Miles Kiefer from talking to anybody!

Still, when he tapped Messenger on the shoulder and the man turned around, he said, "Messenger, I'm Sheriff Kiefer. Like to have a short word with you outside, if you don't mind."

He knew the rate that rumors flew—and grew—among ranch hands, and he didn't want to stoke the furnace any more than he had to.

Outside, he and Messenger stepped around, outside the open parlor window of Charlie Townsend's little house. Charlie might be in there listening, Kiefer figured, but as foreman, he had a right to know what was going on, if anybody did.

"Don't go getting nervous on me, Messenger," Kiefer began. "I'm just curious about what you saw while you were in town these past couple of days."

Messenger shook his head dumbly. "What I saw? I don't get you, Sheriff. What was I supposed to see?"

"Were you anywhere around the hotel yesterday?" Kiefer insisted. "Around the time when David Chandler was shot?"

Messenger hesitated for a moment. Kiefer didn't know what he expected Messenger to say. A blurted confession, maybe? That was highly unlikely, even if the son of a bitch had done it. A long, sad story? Nope. He just didn't know.

At last, Messenger said, "Well, I was about two, maybe three blocks down the street, sittin' and whittlin'. Heard the shot. Saw you drag out that feller a couple minutes later." His eyes narrowed with suspicion. "It's the same feller that's out here, livin' in the big house with Mrs. Chandler, Sheriff."

What was hanging in the air now was an accusation, but it wasn't aimed at the man Kiefer had planned on. It was aimed at *him*!

He said, "Don't get all in an uproar, Messenger. Slocum didn't do it. Leastwise, the evidence right now doesn't point to him. The man I was asking about was you."

Messenger's look turned momentarily into a glare, then quickly quieted back to passivity. "Told you all I know, Sheriff. And what makes you think Slocum didn't do it, all of a sudden?"

"We found his slug, buried in the wall of the building across the alley. He was shooting at a man at the window. A man who was aiming at the Chandlers."

Messenger's brow creased again. "A second man?"

Kiefer nodded. "And a third. The slug that killed Chandler came from Slocum's direction, all right, but I got a witness who'll state that it was delivered by a fella standing behind Slocum a few feet. Maybe on the stairs. Fella who looked a good bit like you, as a matter of fact."

Messenger shook his head. "You got me real confused, Sheriff, I gotta admit."

Kiefer was pretty sure he had his man, he felt it in his gut, but he sadly shook his noggin. "Me, too. But I've got to get her figured out. I'm asking everybody questions, Messenger. Don't feel singled out."

Messenger began, "Well, I—"

The roar of a gun split the evening's silence, and Messenger suddenly looked terribly surprised, buckled over, then fell to the ground.

Kiefer bent down to him in a flash, realizing as he did that the shot had come through Charlie's window, and that Charlie was shouting, "Is everybody all right out there?"

Even as Kiefer knelt to Messenger and saw the life drain from his eyes, he heard Charlie's boot steps echo on the floorboards as he raced to the front door, then across the porch. "Oh, my Christ, my Lord!" he shouted. "I was cleanin' my gun, and she just went off! Sheriff Kiefer! Miles Kiefer! Are you all right?"

23

Slocum took off running at the sound of the shot, with Lil following breathlessly on his heels.

What they found was Charlie Townsend, Miles Kiefer, and the body of Bill Messenger. Lil was so relieved that she almost burst into hysterical laughter, but she dug her nails into her palms, staving it off.

"What the hell happened?" Slocum demanded.

"Accident," said the sheriff, taking off his hat to rub his scalp. "Charlie, here, was inside, cleaning his gun and it went off. By chance, the shot came through the window and hit Messenger, here."

Lil didn't think the sheriff looked all that certain about the accident part—and she couldn't read Charlie's face at all—but she didn't say anything. So long as Messenger wasn't around to cause her problems, it was really none of her business who had killed him or why it had come to pass.

Finally, she had the presence of mind to innocently ask, "Who was he? Did he work here?"

"Just hired him on today," Charlie spoke up. "He was supposed to be quite a bronc buster." His voice broke. "Damn it, anyhow!"

"How terrible!" Lil echoed.

"Charlie," said Slocum, "can I see that gun you were cleanin'?"

Charlie looked up, his face a mask of umbrage. But he quickly erased it and said, "Sure, sure. C'mon inside. Criminy, I feel just awful!" He stopped and turned back toward Kiefer. "Miles, you gonna haul me in?"

"No, Charlie," the sheriff replied. "Don't worry about it."

But Lil didn't think he looked all that certain.

Nonetheless, Charlie said, "Thanks, Miles. You're a good man."

"Doesn't mean there won't be an inquiry, Charlie," the sheriff shouted as Slocum and Charlie went in the door and out of Lil's view.

Inside, all the paraphernalia of gun cleaning was in its proper place. And the weapon in question lay on the table next to it; the faintest hint of smoke still curled about the muzzle in the stillness. The little house smelled of gun oil and smoke.

"She just went off," repeated Charlie. "Just went off. That ain't happened to me in years and years. I feel lower than a well digger's boot, swear to God I do!"

"And you should," muttered Slocum. "You just took a man's life, accident or not."

Charlie sat down in his rocking chair, his head in his hands. "Good Lord, forgive me," he wailed, "God forgive me!"

Slocum picked up the gun and turned it over in his hands, then checked the cylinder. Four slugs, no waiting. If Charlie was like most hands, he'd load only five of the six chambers, so just four cartridges remaining made sense.

Still, it didn't sit right with Slocum. In theory, the hammer should have been resting on an empty chamber. Always.

And in theory, Charlie should have removed the cylinder before he did *anything* else.

If, as he'd claimed, he'd really been cleaning the gun.

Slocum set the gun back down on the table and said, "Thanks, Charlie."

Charlie didn't answer. He just sat there with his head in his hands.

Slocum let himself out the front door. Lil was still standing where he'd left her—staring at the body—and Kiefer had gone off somewhere. Probably to find somebody to help him with the corpse.

"Kiefer go to get a couple of the hands?" he asked Lil.

"And he said something about a wagon," she replied.

"Should've waited to send ours back," he muttered and cast a glance toward the barn.

"What?" Lil asked, then said, "Oh. Never mind." She looked as though the event had drained her heavily. Well, why shouldn't it? It wasn't often one was that close to two murders in two days.

But still, she seemed more upset about Messenger's demise than she had about her husband's.

Odd.

He slid his arm around her shoulders. "I think you'd better finish your dinner, gal."

She said, "Yes, Slocum," rather limply and turned to go back to the house.

Lil closed the door behind her and leaned back against it, blowing out air through pursed lips. Of all the dumb luck!

Still, it had been quite a shock, seeing Bill lying there on the ground, dead. More than she'd thought it would be, back when she was trying to plan his demise. He'd always been so full of life.

How strange and bizarre that he'd fallen victim to an accident just when he had. After all, he'd likely come here to kill her. Expose her, at the very least.

And it was probably Bill who'd shot and killed David yesterday.

A little chill ran through her, and she rubbed at her arms. *He's dead now,* she told herself. *He can't hurt you or anybody else, anymore.*

And then she realized how silly that was. He'd probably never hurt so much as a fly in his life, until she'd conned him. She'd made out pretty well on that one, she reminded herself.

Well, he'd just been asking for it, being so rich and so gullible and all . . .

She stood up straight, walked to the dining room

table, and seated herself. She also served herself another enchilada before Slocum had a second chance at them.

She poured herself a second cup of coffee, too, and as she did, she began to hum some nameless tune. Despite all the hubbub, she was suddenly feeling almost chipper. She had the money, she had Slocum—for a little while, anyway—and she was rid of Bill Messenger for good and all.

She was the cat who'd swallowed the canary, and she knew it.

Slocum answered the knock at the door this time. It was Miles Kiefer again.

He said, "Slocum, we got the body loaded in a wagon, but I'm thinking that it's getting late, and I'm not much in favor of driving a rig all the way back to town when it's this dark." He pointed up, indicating the faint crescent moon.

Slocum nodded. It would throw a wrench into his plans for the evening, but he threw the door the rest of the way open and said, "You're welcome to stay over, Kiefer."

But the sheriff shook his head. "No. I'll be just fine in the bunkhouse. But I'm tellin' you that Cookie isn't any too handy with a stove. If you've got any leftovers . . ."

Slocum laughed. "Sure, sure. C'mon in. We were just cleanin' up."

Miles stepped inside, and Lil herself served him

dinner while Slocum sat at the far end of the table, smoking. David Chandler had had good taste in cigars, and Slocum had found his humidor.

"You know," Kiefer said, when Lil was out in the kitchen, "between you and me and the fence post, Chandler wasn't any angel. Miss Lil was probably lucky he got killed when he did."

Slocum scowled, midpuff. "What you mean?"

"I mean that Chandler wasn't his real name."

Slocum gave a shrug. "That, I know. I told you about it, remember?"

"Oh, right." Kiefer continued, chancing a quick look toward the kitchen, "Sorry. But it was robbery, murder, you name it. Killed your friend, you said. But, so long as a man keeps his nose clean in my town, I ain't got no grudge against him. I'll watch him close, but that's it. Until he tries to pull something, anyhow."

"I guess Chandler didn't try to pull anything in Poleaxe?"

"That's right," Kiefer replied and took a large bite of enchilada. "Damn, these are good, Slocum! You make this?"

Slocum ignored the question. He merely picked up his cigar again, rolled the ash off against the china, and stuck it in his mouth.

Around another mouthful of enchilada, Kiefer mumbled, "If this is your idea of campfire cookin', I'll ride with you anytime . . ."

"I been thinkin', Kiefer," Slocum said. "I'm wonderin' if you got any paper on Messenger back at the office."

"Any paper? On Messenger?"

"Current, or old, maybe," Slocum said. "Just wonderin', you know? And another thing. How well do you know this Charlie Townsend?"

Kiefer put down his fork. "Why?"

"Because I don't think that shootin' was any accident."

Kiefer's brow furrowed. "Charlie's been in Poleaxe since before I came. Hell, he used to own this ranch until Chandler bought him out!"

"He did?" Slocum's mind really started into spinning, now.

"Oh, sure. I wonder how he's gonna take to having a lady boss. Never been one for the ladies, has Charlie. Always figured him for a woman hater, as a matter of fact."

"No accountin' for some feller's tastes," said Slocum, and blew a smoke ring.

"Oh, I don't mean nothing like that," Kiefer added quickly. "I always just figured that somewhere along the line, a woman did him wrong in a real big way. He just doesn't trust any of them. I remember one time—before Chandler came to town—we had a couple of nuns come through on their way to the mission, down south. One of their horses went lame, and they tried to buy one from Charlie. He charged 'em double, said they looked sneaky to him."

"Nuns?" Slocum nearly choked. "Sneaky?"

"Nuns," replied Kiefer, with a nod. "Damnedest thing I ever heard of. I mean, I wouldn't even have expected that kind of horseshit out of Jess!"

Slocum laughed, and said, "By Christ!"

24

The sheriff had retired to the bunkhouse, Lil was back down the hall, unpacking, and Slocum sat in the parlor, smoking his second cigar and drinking a glass of the late David Chandler's port. It was pretty damned good port, too.

If you liked port, which Slocum really didn't. But it seemed that Chandler hadn't kept anything else around the place.

He was thinking over the information that had come to him tonight, which, all in all, was a whole lot. Too much to digest at once, almost. But he did his best.

This used to be Charlie's place, which gave Charlie a pretty damned good reason to take a shot at Chandler—especially since Kiefer said that Charlie hated women, and, well, Chandler was marrying a woman with a capital *W* in Lily.

That might have been just enough to push him over the edge.

But if Charlie had been in the hotel for the wedding, surely somebody would have recognized him. And he didn't match Mrs. Tinny's description, not at all.

Bill Messenger did, however. He wondered if the sheriff had noticed. Probably. Kiefer didn't strike him as being slow off the mark.

Again, Slocum wondered about Lil's past, and if Messenger had anything to do with it. Of course, she hadn't given herself away if indeed, he had, but then, Lil was a con woman. She wouldn't go all to pieces and just holler out, "Oh my God, I'm married to him." Or engaged, or, "I took him for thirty grand," or whatever.

No, Lil was the Queen of Lies. Always had been, always would be.

He stubbed out his cigar, stood up, and walked down the hall. He went to Lil's room, where he found her suitcases lined up on the bed and Lil, herself, sitting on the floor before her open trunk.

"Hello, darling!" she chirped when she saw him.

"Just wanted to tell you," he said. "I'm goin' to bed."

"Oh! Well, pull those valises off the mattress, then, and—"

"Told you, honey. I ain't gonna sleep in a dead man's room."

Her brows knitted prettily. "Very well, then. I'll be there in a minute."

He grunted and went back to the room they'd used before. He lit the lamps and pulled the shades down and stripped out of his clothes. The sheets felt nice and cool, better than the linens at the hotel. David Chandler hadn't skimped on anything, he guessed. At least, he'd bet anything that ol' Charlie Townsend hadn't had stuff this nice in the house when it was his.

Charlie Townsend sat in his parlor, waiting. His lights were out, and he stared up toward his late boss's room. The bitch had the lamp lit but hadn't pulled the shade. He could tell that by the strength of the light spilling out, but he couldn't see more. From this angle, the window appeared like a mere slit in the house.

He'd thought about going and looking out the bedroom window, but why? He didn't give a damn what she was doing in there, so long as she was there.

Again, he picked up his gun, feeling the cool reassurance of its metal, the solidity of its ebony grip. He'd hoped to kill that nosy sheriff earlier, but he'd hit the new hand instead. Well, it couldn't be helped, he supposed.

He'd had to shoot from back here, where he'd be sitting if he were really cleaning his gun, as he'd claimed, and had to aim for the sound of the men's voices, rather than the actual sight of them.

All things considered, it was pretty much a miracle he'd hit anybody.

He'd have done better if he'd had his rifle, though. He was better with a rifle.

But his shoulder reminded him why he hadn't relied on the other weapon. Slocum's slug had pierced him only an inch away from where the long gun nestled into his shoulder, and it still hurt like hell. He'd put up a good front before the other men today, but it pained him something fierce.

At least his face was almost completely healed. The only way he could find the cuts amid the wrinkles on his face was to feel for them. The glass had been thin and sharp, and although they'd bled like a son of a bitch, once he'd gotten them cleaned up, the wounds had practically disappeared.

He congratulated himself on his luck—for not the first time—and took another look toward David Chandler's window. The situation was unchanged. The lights were undimmed.

"Might's well have a cup'a coffee," he muttered, and went to refill his empty mug. "Bitch is sure takin' her own sweet time. Don't she ever get sleepy?"

Lil, having retreated to the front of her room to change into a nightgown—a green one, which really set off her hair, she thought—walked back to pull down the shade of her window. Best not advertise to the rest of the ranch that she wasn't sleeping in here, but with Slocum. That is, if "the rest of the ranch" ever came around to this side of the house.

For the sake of tidiness, she threw a coverlet over her bags, leaving them on the bed, then bent to blow out her lamp. Closing the door behind her, she padded softly to Slocum's room, rapped on the door to announce herself, then let herself in.

It was dark inside, but she remembered where the bed was and made her way to it. Just before she reached it, though, a large hand snaked around her fanny and pinched her left buttock.

"'Bout time you got here, girl," came Slocum's baritone rumble. He pulled her to him, and she tumbled onto the bed—and him.

"You don't have any lights lit," she purred as she wriggled into a more comfortable position. "I wanted you to see my nightgown."

His fingers undid the little ribbon that tied it at the front. "I'll see it in the morning."

"It won't be the same," she whispered hoarsely as she felt the gown fall down to her waist, felt his hand cup first one breast, then the other, then felt the moist heat of his lips and tongue upon her nipple.

"Um," Slocum said. The sound rumbled through her bosom and radiated through her body, nearly toppling her over the edge, and she gasped.

This time, he chuckled, her nipple still caught between his teeth, and the vibrating sound, following so closely on the heels of the first, pushed her directly into an orgasm.

She seized in his arms, crying his name.

He held her until she stopped trembling, and then he shifted her, removing the gown completely and pushing back the bed linens. He was naked beneath them, and he rolled on top of her, his legs between hers. Nothing had ever felt so good as Slocum, naked, mounting her.

She spread her legs farther and threw her arms around his neck, kissing him deeply.

He returned it, embellished it, and as he did, he slid himself inside her. She knew she was wet, for he met no resistance, and he began to move slowly, rhythmically.

Her light was finally out.

Charlie Townsend eased himself out his bedroom window and landed softly on the dirt outside. Keeping low, he crept across the darkened lot to her window.

The shade was pulled, but the window itself was open. Gingerly, he pushed aside the shade a little using two fingers. He couldn't see much, but he could make out a shape on the bed.

She was a lot fatter under that coverlet than she looked in clothes, that was for sure.

He brought up his gun and aimed it at her. He couldn't see her head, so he aimed for her back. At this range, his slug could sever her spine and go right through the heart, if he was lucky.

Maybe.

He studied on it a little more.

He'd only have the time for one shot, he knew that. He wanted to make it count.

Stinking bitch. She wasn't going to take over things, not if he had anything to say about it!

He'd halfway given up on getting the ranch back. That had been a stupid idea. Where did he think he'd get the money? But still, he wasn't going to work for some hussy who strutted the stage!

He took careful aim through the gloom, or at least, as careful as he could.

He fired.

Caught in the throes of orgasm, it took Slocum a half second to figure out that the loud noise he'd just heard was a gunshot, and a close one, too. Beneath him, Lil had stopped her spasms and turned her head dumbly toward the sound.

Slocum clambered off of her and jerked open the shade. There was nothing in the side lot, although he thought he saw some movement over at the caretaker's cottage. But Charlie might have come to the window at the sound, just as he had.

"Stay down," he whispered to Lil, and he grabbed his britches and gun as he crawled out of bed. He had his pants on by the time he made it to the hall, and his gun belt strapped over them before he entered Lil's room.

There wasn't much to see in the dark, but he made out a little spray of gunpowder at the edge of the shade. Someone had fired from there, and doubtless into the room from the outside.

Thank God Lil had been with him!

He went to the bed, struck a match, and discovered a neat round hole piercing the coverlet Lil had tossed over her line of bags. From the window, the shooter had mistaken the valises for a sleeping body.

He shook out the match and went back to Lil. He was certain now that the bullet that had killed Chandler hadn't been meant for him. Lil had been the target, all along.

Halfway into his room, somebody pounded on the front door. "Get yourself decent," he whispered to Lil, and left.

Charlie Townsend was on the front porch, followed momentarily by Miles Kiefer, who was trying to run and button his shirt and buckle his gun belt all at the same time.

"What was it? Who shot who?" Charlie demanded.

"What he said," cried Kiefer. "Is everybody all right in there?"

Slocum swung wide the door and let them pile in. He said, "Nobody's hurt, unless you count one of Miss Lily's satchels."

Charlie's face screwed up. "What? One'a her bags?"

"That's right," Slocum answered. "Want to come back and take a look? I'll show you." He knew he wasn't giving Lil much time, but she was good at thinking on her feet. In her business, she had to be.

that fella I saw down to the livery the other day? The one just sittin' out there, watching from the crest of the rise?"

"Yeah?" replied Kiefer, distracted.

"You thinkin' what I'm thinkin'?"

"If you mean, was he the one who took that shot at Chandler later on, yeah," Kiefer said.

"And he was Charlie Townsend," added Slocum.

Kiefer nodded curtly. "Makes sense to me." He pulled aside the curtains on one side of the door and snuck a slanted look outside. "Don't see him."

"Probably went to the barn, or back to his house," said Slocum. He moved to the window on the other side and peeked out the curtains. "I don't see him, either."

"Don't mean he isn't sitting out there somewhere, with his rifle across his knees."

"Well, let's just hope he keeps it across his knees," said Slocum, and with a rebel yell, swung open the front door.

Lil jumped at Slocum's wild holler and clung to the doorway, peeking around the edge. All she saw was Kiefer's back as the two men plunged outside.

She was scared, as scared as she had ever been. She knew her life was actually in grave danger, and almost worse, that Slocum's was. Not that she'd perish if Slocum were to be killed, but it would surely break her heart. For at least a week or two.

She looked around for a place to hide and finally scooted beneath the bed, along with the dust balls and cobwebs. She held her breath.

Kiefer headed for the barn, and Slocum headed for the foreman's house, shoving aside cowhands wakened by the noise. They told everybody to get back to the bunkhouse, but if they saw Charlie, to detain him.

Slocum added that he was armed and dangerous, and belatedly, Kiefer did, too.

Before Slocum made it to the first step, a shot rang through Townsend's front window, and Slocum hit the dirt, rolling. And he realized, as he did, that Townsend had clipped his shoulder. Pain radiated from it, but as far as he could tell, nothing was broken.

He began to crawl along the side of the house.

Kiefer did an about-face and ran, crouching, in his direction. Slocum signaled him to go to the other side of Townsend's house, which he did.

Once Kiefer was in the clear, Slocum crawled back farther, until he reached the second window. Then slowly, his shoulder burning like the wrong end of a branding iron, he pulled himself up the side of the house until he could peek over the sill.

Townsend was in there, all right, and he had a rifle in his hands. He was pacing like a chained dog. Gone was the final doubt that he was the killer. Maybe he hadn't killed David Chandler, but he'd shot at him the day before, and he'd shot at Lil, and now Slocum. That made him plenty dangerous.

It made him fair game.

Slocum brought up his gun and leveled it at Townsend's pacing figure. Or rather, his shadow. There were no lights lit in the room, and the only illumination came through the drawn curtains. Weak, at best.

Still, Slocum could make out his form. He squeezed the trigger.

And was heartily surprised when an answering blast, almost simultaneous, ripped through the wall boards, slicing a hole in his side.

He fell to the ground again, groaning, and heard Kiefer's "Holy shit!" coming from the other side of the abode.

Another rifle shot split the air, and then Slocum heard something hit the ground, which he assumed was Kiefer.

Damn!

Slocum gingerly felt his side. There was a lot of blood, but he was fairly sure that Townsend had hit nothing but meat. Considering the circumstances, it didn't much matter one way or the other.

He had to take Townsend out.

Kiefer gritted his teeth against the pain emanating from his head. He thought he'd lost consciousness for a minute or two, but how many minutes, really? One? Two? Five? Ten?

There was no way of knowing.

For the second time, he wiped the flood of blood

from his brow and looked around for his hat, which he finally spied twenty feet out, in the weeds.

Well, that would have to wait.

Slocum was counting on him. And more importantly, the entire town of Poleaxe was counting on him. Kiefer took his job seriously, and it would take more than getting his skull grazed to change that.

He began to crawl forward, toward the front of the house again, keeping his moves as silent as possible. Townsend was aiming at sounds, now. And he realized, just then, that Townsend had probably known just exactly who he was shooting when Messenger was killed.

Which meant that Messenger, for whatever reason, was more than likely the galoot who'd slain David Chambers.

Kiefer didn't claim to understand it. He just figured it was up to him to stop it—hopefully, with Slocum.

But he'd do it alone if he had to.

26

Charlie figured to be sitting in the catbird seat.

He'd wounded both of them. It was just a matter of time.

He didn't think about "his" ranch. He didn't think about anything except those two men out there, the ones he was killing, a little bit at a time.

It was like the war. He'd always been his best at wartime.

He listened carefully, hardly daring to breathe. Kiefer was making his way back toward the front of the house, he was fairly certain. Slocum was a little noisier, since he fell from time to time, and was going back, along the side of the house toward the rear.

He must be hit worse than Kiefer. He was inching.

Townsend decided to take out Slocum first. The man was a legend, but even legends could be killed, he thought with a smile.

He tiptoed down the short hall to the next window from which Slocum might strike.

Slocum bypassed the next window and went around to the rear of the house, keeping his balance—and his feet beneath him. For a change.

But he'd been wrong. There was no rear door, only a high, single-paned window.

He grimaced. He'd have to make do.

He slowly pulled himself fully upright, just at the side of the window, his gun ready. He chanced a glance inside.

He saw darkness, and in that darkness, the shadow of a man just disappearing through a side door in the hallway.

Damn!

Despite the pain, he held his position, the blood from his side and shoulder flowing down the side of the house in slow rivulets.

Miles Kiefer had crept silently to the front of the house. And waited, listening for the slightest sound from inside. If Townsend could aim at sounds, he figured he could, too. Maybe he wouldn't hit much of anything, but he could try.

But he hadn't heard a peep, and now he was considering crawling up on the porch. Except that Charlie's porch squeaked in spots, if he remembered right. Shit.

His head dropped to the ground, giving him a quick and painful reminder of his wound, and he jerked it back up. The far side of the house, then. Maybe Slocum was still there. Maybe he'd have an idea.

He started crawling again.

* * *

Slocum wavered in and out of consciousness, but somehow he remained standing, propped up by the side of the house. He knew he was losing too much blood to keep upright much longer, but there wasn't a damned thing he could do about it, not without making a sound, not without alerting Townsend to his presence.

And then he had an idea. It was a desperate one, but it was the only one he had handy.

He fired through the window, breaking the glass, and immediately threw himself to the side. When Townsend returned fire, he emptied his gun into the clapboards, toward the sound, then quickly reloaded.

And Kiefer was on the ball. When Slocum stopped to reload, he began to fire, getting off his last shot just as Slocum was ready to start again.

This time, Slocum sprayed his slugs farther apart. There was no answering gunfire.

But Townsend was tricky. He knew that. So he reloaded and waited.

It seemed that the sheriff was waiting, too. A moment later, Kiefer poked his head around the corner of the building and waved to get Slocum's attention. He'd been shot in the head—or scalp, more like, and blood covered his face and ear. He gestured, as if to ask what the hell was going on, and Slocum could only shrug. The pain of movement reminded him of his shoulder, and he turned away, listening intently.

Suddenly, Curly was standing there, as if he'd come from nowhere, and he asked, in a loud voice, "Ain't you gonna go in and take a look-see?"

At which point, another shot came from the house, and Curly toppled to the ground.

He wasn't dead, but he was moaning. Kiefer crawled over to silence him, but Slocum emptied his gun, once more, into the house's walls.

A slug burst through the siding, and Slocum felt a whoosh of air as it passed by, but he was untouched.

He reloaded and fired again. This time, he heard a heavy thud. A body, hitting the floor.

He kept listening, waiting to hear Townsend crawling or trying to right himself, but he heard nothing. It seemed that Townsend was either dead or at least out cold. He had to act fast.

He pushed himself to his feet and started back around, toward the front, bypassing Kiefer who still knelt over Curly.

"He's down," he whispered as he passed by.

"Be careful," Kiefer whispered in reply.

The words weren't wasted on Slocum, although they weren't really necessary. He moved around to the porch, peeked into the front window, and saw nothing.

He opened the front door. Still, no retaliation.

He lit a candle and held it in his left hand, far out in front of him. His gun was in his right, and ready.

He and Kiefer had done a good bit of damage to the inside of Townsend's house, all right. Moonlight seeped in through various holes in the walls, and the furniture was peppered with slugs. Some of the wooden stuff, including an old rocker, was splintered.

Slocum made his way down the hall. He was still barefoot, so his steps were silent. He just hoped that if Townsend was down there, waiting for him, he'd shoot for the candlelight.

Still, no sign. He could see the little window he'd broken with his first shot, and the doorway he'd seen Townsend disappear into. This was it.

Holding the candle ahead of his body, Slocum stepped into the doorway, gun ready.

What he found was Townsend, sprawled on the floor of the kitchen. He'd been hit several times, and if he wasn't dead, he was close to it.

Slocum kicked the gun from his hand and shouted, "It's clear, Kiefer!"

He heard Kiefer shouting to one of the other hands to come and help Curly, and then the sheriff's footsteps as they rounded the house and came across the front porch and into the parlor.

"Back here," Slocum said.

"Right."

And then Kiefer stood beside him, over Charlie Townsend's body. "Dead?" asked Kiefer.

"Or near to it."

Kiefer took the candle, then knelt to the body, turning it over.

"Seven slugs in him, all told. And the son of a bitch is still breathing."

"Sometimes there's just no figurin' on the Lord's will," Slocum said softly. "How's Curly?"

"He'll live."

"Good."

"Wanna help haul him to the parlor?"

Slocum grunted, then picked up Townsend's feet. Between them, they just managed to get Townsend down the hall and to the parlor floor. They were both still bleeding quite a bit, and Slocum slumped down on the old divan.

"We'd best go do something about these wounds," Kiefer said as he wiped the blood out of his eyes. Again. "I'll send for Cookie to watch him."

Slocum nodded. "Fine by me." He struggled to stand up again, and started out the front door while Kiefer shouted for Cookie to come, and on the double.

Slocum stumbled, at long last, into the main house and called for Lil. At least, he thought he did.

The last thing he truly recalled was opening the front door and falling into the house, face-first.

When Kiefer came in a few minutes later, he nearly tripped over Slocum. He wasn't feeling any too well himself, and he got to a chair before he hollered, "Miz Chandler! We could use some help out here!"

A moment later, he heard rustling, and a moment after that, heard her bare feet pad up the hall.

She entered the parlor, took one look at Slocum's fallen form, and without sparing a glance for the sheriff, went straight to his side, murmuring, "Slocum, Slocum, no!"

Kiefer closed his eyes at last. He figured she'd get to him.

Eventually.

When he woke, the dawn was just breaking, and his head was bandaged. Mrs. Chandler's beautiful face looked down upon him.

"About time, Sheriff," she said.

"What happened while I was out?"

"I stitched you up and cleaned you up, and got you bandaged. I put some salve on that cut, too. You're lucky it didn't do more than crease your skull."

"Thanks," he said. "But I meant, what happened with Slocum? And Charlie Townsend?"

"Don't worry about it. Slocum's going to be just fine, and that vile Charlie Townsend died during the night," she said. "Honestly, I don't know what gets into men sometimes! Why do you think he did it, Sheriff?"

"You've got me there, ma'am," he said, and it was the truth. He still didn't understand it.

But at least the case was closed. To his satisfaction, anyhow. He'd take a few slugs for Poleaxe, but enough was enough.

"What'd they do with Townsend's body?" he asked, and groaned when he sat up.

"Put it in the wagon with that other poor unfortunate, I'd suppose," she replied. She looked like an angel, and for a moment, he forgot what Slocum had told him about her past.

"I'd best go see to them," he said. "Best be getting back to town, too."

"Wait and have some breakfast," she said. "Some coffee, at least. Slocum's awake, and he'll be out in a minute."

"Maybe just some coffee . . ." Kiefer said grudgingly and stood up.

Mrs. Chandler took his arm and helped him to the table, sat him down, and brought him a fresh cup of coffee and a plate of fried eggs. "I'm sorry I'm not a better cook, Sheriff."

Around a mouthful of eggs he hadn't thought he wanted, he said, "Mighty fine, ma'am, mighty fine."

Slocum stumbled down the hall at about the same time the sheriff finished his breakfast. He was still without his shirt—although he'd put his boots back on—and his shoulder was bandaged, as well as his side. Blood and fluid had seeped through the bandages on his side, soaking it.

Using the backs of chairs for balance, he made his way to the table and sat down at its head. "Mornin', Kiefer," he muttered hoarsely. "Lil?"

She poked her head out of the kitchen. "Be right there, Slocum."

She was, with another plate of eggs and another cup of coffee. This time, she went back into the kitchen and fetched the pot.

Which she did not offer to Kiefer.

He shrugged it off, then stood and pushed his chair back in. "I'm off, then. Want to thank you folks for a real interesting night."

Slocum gave a halfhearted laugh. "Any time, Kiefer."

And with that, he left to ferry the dead back to town.

27

Once the sheriff had driven the wagon out of the yard, Slocum said, "You knew that man, didn't you, Lil?"

Her face all innocence, she said, "What man is that, Slocum?"

"The man that was killed first. Messenger."

"What makes you think—?"

"Come off it, Lil. He fit the description of the man behind me in the lobby. The one who shot Chandler. And who was probably aiming at you. Was he one of your marks, Lily?"

She looked down, tracing the pattern in the tablecloth with a finger. "All right. You guessed it, Slocum. I was married to him."

Slocum closed his eyes. Lil was like a beloved dog you couldn't bring yourself to put down or give away, no matter how many chickens she killed, no matter how many pairs of britches she tore up, no matter how many boots she chewed on.

"But it was a long time ago, Slocum," she added lamely.

"Don't matter how long ago it was, Lil," he said. "The point is, he came after you. You don't know how many others there are out there, just waitin' for a chance." He took a long, thoughtful drink of his coffee. It wasn't bad, considering that Lil had made it.

"Here's the deal, Lil darlin'," he said. "You've got to cut it out. You've got to know when enough is enough. Otherwise, it's gonna get somebody else on your track, and I won't be around to save your bacon."

She just stared at him.

He stared back for a time, as if to ram home his point, but when he didn't get any reaction, he turned his attention to his breakfast. Fine, let her get herself killed. He just hoped she wouldn't take too many other people with her.

But then she broke the silence. "I've already decided to stop, Slocum. This was my last con, for good and all. I'm going up to San Francisco. Going to settle down."

He lowered his fork. "I'm right pleased to hear that, Lil, right pleased. You've made an old saddle tramp real happy."

She slid into the chair on his right. "I know this is asking a lot. I mean, I know it's practically impossible. But . . . Slocum, would you consider coming . . . with me?"

He grinned at her. "I reckon I could spare you a week or two, Lil, but—"

"But your feet get to itching," she said with a sad smile. "I understand." She brightened. "I'll take what I can get, though. Consider it a deal."

Slocum winked at her, then turned back to his

eggs. If he'd been another man—or maybe the same man, but at a different time—he might have taken her up on it. But right then, he wasn't a man who could live on the proceeds of a woman's larceny, nor was he a man who could stay in one place very long.

He was glad she understood.

"You make any toast?" he asked.

Back in town, Miles Kiefer had made his drop-off at the undertaker's and was already at his desk. He put off writing reports, however, to go back through the old wanted posters. He kept a couple boxes of them in the extra cell.

There was nothing in the first box, but lo and behold, halfway through the second he came across a worn handbill for Bill Messenger. He was wanted for attempting to stick up a stagecoach. After that single flyer, there was no more paper on him.

Kiefer sniffed and went back to his desk. He could write some letters and track Messenger's record later. Right now, he had to make enough sense of what had happened last night to write it up for the files.

He wasn't much looking forward to it.

Lil rolled toward him on the bed, and rested her chin on his chest.

"Slocum?"

He opened one eye. "What can I do for you? That I haven't already, I mean," he said with a sly grin.

She playfully slugged his arm. "Oh, you!"

"Sorry," he said, chuckling. "What is it?"

"I've been thinking."

"Sounds dangerous."

"No, really. I have. When I go on to San Francisco, and you come along—"

"For a week or so."

"Right," she said reluctantly. "Well, wouldn't you, couldn't you try to—"

Gently, he put his hand on her back. "No, darlin'. I can't. That's not the way things are."

"But if you stayed with me . . . Just think how it could be! The Barbary Coast could be your pearl! The theater, the opera—"

"Opera?" he snorted. "You're dreamin', baby."

"All right, then," she said. "Champagne sold on every corner, practically! The finest cigars! And me, waiting for you every night in a nice, soft, warm bed."

He played with a russet strand of silky hair. As nice as she made it sound, Panther and a stretch of open desert called to him more insistently.

"Sounds tempting, but no. Don't push it, Lily. Please."

She sighed deeply. "I had to try. It's just . . . how I am going to do it without you, Slocum?"

He frowned. "Do what?"

"Live this . . . straight life! Be an upstanding citizen! I don't know how."

He hugged her. "Oh, you'll remember, Lil. It's been a while, but you'll remember and be fine."

"No, I won't. I've never been straight and legal, not since before I was born!"

"Afraid you lost me, there, Lil."

"I mean that even before I was born, my mother was turning cons. Daddy, too. I didn't pick this trade, Slocum, I was born into it. My real name is Rhiannon Escobar. My daddy was a Spanish gypsy—worked fake fortune-telling and the badger game, mostly—and Mama was an Irish sneak thief and the next thing to a prostitute. If I hadn't had talent, I'd probably still be back in New York, turning tricks at Five Corners."

"Lil," he began, but she cut him off.

"No, I wanted to tell you, Slocum. It's my way of . . . begging, I guess."

"Baby, listen. You don't need to beg from me or anybody else. Look how far you've come already! My, God, Lil! You'll be fine. You'll land on your feet. You always do, you know."

She began to cry.

He pulled her closer, saying, "Shh, shh, it's all right, Lily. It's all right." He kissed her brow. "I've seen this happen before, honey."

She sniffed. "You have?"

"You've had a dream all your life," he continued. He supposed crooks could have dreams, too. "And now, that dream is coming true. That was one thing you didn't really allow for, was it, that it would actually happen? And I'll bet you didn't plan beyond it."

She nipped at his chest, and he shouted, "Ouch! What was that for?"

"For being so smart. You know, I think you're exactly right. I just don't have a plan. I never did. For the happily-ever-after part, I mean."

"You're the cleverest gal I ever met, Lil," he said with a smile. "You'll come up with something that'll shake the world right down to its shoes."

She lifted her head and looked up at him, smiling, although her eyes still brimmed with unspilled tears. "I will, won't I?"

He kissed her.

JAKE LOGAN
TODAY'S HOTTEST ACTION WESTERN!

Explore the exciting Old West with one of the men who made it wild!

**AVAILABLE WHEREVER BOOKS ARE SOLD OR AT
PENGUIN.COM**

(Ad # B112)

J. R. ROBERTS

THE GUNSMITH